Corruption of an Innocent Girl

J.W. MCKENNA

CORRUPTION OF AN INNOCENT GIRL
AND OTHER EROTIC TALES

2008

Corruption of an Innocent Girl

INDEX

OTHER BOOKS BY J.W. MCKENNA

* Available in print as well as ebook form.
See www.jwmckenna.com

CORRUPTION OF AN INNOCENT GIRL

CHAPTER ONE

Jason Reynolds didn't know what to do with himself. As a member of the "idle rich," he could do just about anything he wanted—fly to Rio for the carnival, attend the heavyweight title fight in Vegas, or jet to Hollywood to visit some of his celebrity friends. There was just one problem: He was fresh out of rehab and hoping to stay sober.

Among his wealthy peers, being "dry" was tantamount to having leprosy. How can you have a good time when you can't order Cristal by the case or swill mimosas for breakfast? And more to the point: How can you pick up women without liquor as your crutch? Jason knew he wasn't exactly good-looking. He was a bit short and heavy around the middle, and his eyes were too close together, giving his face a pinched look. Alcohol had made him feel much more attractive.

No one had forced him into rehab. Well, not exactly. His drunkenness lasted an even dozen years, from his days fresh out of high school until his crash and burn at the New Year's Eve debacle, when he was arrested for trying to fondle female revelers in Times Square. His lawyers got him off, of course, and his father strongly suggested he enter rehab.

"You embarrass this family too much and your grandpa might just decide to leave all his money to charity," his father had warned. That would sober up any rich drunk, Jason decided. The incident occurred during a down period of his life, when he had been thinking about his wasted youth and looking ahead to more of the same. He decided, now that he had hit thirty, it was time to grow up a little.

He entered a sixty-day program and it surprised him that he completed the damn thing. He'd even received kudos from the staff—and from his conservative family. It had been very difficult, but looking back, he was glad he did it.

Now what?

He couldn't hang around with his drunken friends. By now, even Jason had realized that those people weren't really his friends. They were suck-ups and sycophants, boozers and losers, and for the most part, he was well rid of them. What he really needed, he told himself, was to hang around regular people—working stiffs.

Except he didn't know any regular people. Not only that, he'd been looking down on regular people since he could first talk and he found it difficult to treat them any differently just because he was sober. It was a real dilemma.

What's more, as a newly sober rich person, he was able to see, for the first time, just how little respect these working men and women had for people like him. Because he had been drunk most of the time, he missed the rolling of the eyes and the muttered asides. But a sober Jason heard the comments. He quickly discovered they considered people like him "useless," "spoiled," and "stuck-up." Sure, they were envious, but the depth of their distaste had surprised him nonetheless. They wanted little to do with a reformed rich drunk. Unless he was handing out money, in which case they'd be happy to take it from him.

He felt like a man without a peer group.

Currently ensconced in a top-floor suite of the Bel-Air Hotel in Miami's South Beach this sunny March day, Jason was bored, lonely and antsy. His former friends were currently asleep, waiting for cocktail hour to spring forth and carouse. Like vampires, they'd stay up most of the night. So what was a currently sober dilettante supposed to do at eleven o'clock in the morning?

He rose from his bed and went to take a shower. He had no plan yet, but thought getting dressed might be the first step. Then maybe brunch. It was as far ahead as his mind could think. Standing naked in front of the mirror, Jason pinched a bit of flab around the middle and grimaced. Wouldn't hurt to work out a little, he thought. Fortunately, he hadn't lost his hair. A stocky man with cool gray eyes stared back at him and when he gave himself that lopsided grin, he could imagine girls giving him a second look.

Yeah, drunk girls.

Two hours later, having been well fed and taken a clear-headed walk around the grounds, Jason could feel the first tendrils of a relapse brewing in his mind. *This is boring!* his evil side told him. *Fuck this sober shit—get drunk and join your friends! Maybe pick up a cute girl!*

His good side chimed in: *You don't have to be drunk to get laid. Come on, you're a charming guy!*

"Yeah, that's right!" he told himself out loud, looking around to see if anyone noticed he was suddenly talking to himself.

It wasn't much of a plan, but it would have to do. Find a nice girl, preferably a sober girl, and have some sex. Even his evil twin could get behind that. He went down to the pool and watched the cute babes sun themselves and splash around. Within the first hour, he made three key observations. First, there didn't appear to be any sober women anywhere. They were drinking mai-tais, beers, piòa coladas and martinis—and it was barely afternoon. Second, without alcohol to prop him up, he was really a rather shy man. It took some effort to approach a woman. The old "Can I buy you a drink" line no longer worked.

But his biggest shock came with his final observation, one that alcohol had disguised: The women he met fell into two main categories: The "rich bitches" who were as sleek and high-maintenance as Jaguars, and the "dollar belles," the middle-class secretaries from Kansas or somewhere who were looking for a meal ticket and didn't really care who they ended up with. Without alcohol to dull his senses, he found both types to be repellent and he left his station after a couple of hours to head back to his room.

Alone.

Damn, this sober business is harder than I thought.

He rode up the elevator with a couple from the Midwest—he could always spot them: Pale and heavyset like dumplings, they treated South Beach like Mecca. Both were in their mid-forties and the man sported a sunburn across half his face. But listening to them talk to each other, it was clear they were in love. He glanced over at them, feeling a strange sort of envy. They were having an actual conversation about the world and things that mattered. Compared to some of the conversations he had in the last ten years—What do you want to drink? Wanna go up to my room?—Jason suddenly felt inferior for the first time in his life.

In that moment, his evil twin spoke up, *Yeah, but you're rich. You can buy and sell people like this.*

The doors opened and the couple moved off. As Jason's eyes followed them, he suddenly noticed a pretty Latina maid standing next to her cart in the corridor. She was dressed in the hotel uniform, an ugly pink dress with her nametag above her left breast. Jason figured her to be no more than twenty, with that freshness that young girls exhibit. She had long black hair, tied back in a ponytail and very little makeup. She was busy gathering towels and just as the elevator doors closed, she turned to see him and she flashed him a beautiful smile.

In that split second, Jason knew what he wanted to do. The vision came to him so completely that he actually laughed out loud. He would play a game, one that would show his superiority and expose the venal nature of the so-called "real" people around him. If he couldn't drink and carouse, he could do this. And he would play it with that cute maid he had just seen.

The elevator began to rise and Jason glanced at the floor designation. Eight. Good. He rode up to his floor at twelve and immediately punched the button to return to the eighth floor. He left the elevator and stood by the cart. After a minute, the pretty maid reappeared from the room. She seemed surprised to see him.

"*Si? ¿Se puede ayudar?*"

Hmm, he thought, this could be a problem. "Do you speak English?"

"*Un poco.* A little. I understand okay."

"Great! Uh, what's your name?" He recalled some of his high school Spanish. "*Come se llama?*"

6

"Maria." She smiled.

Of course she'd be named Maria, he thought. He reached into his pocket and felt the wad of cash there. Immediately, he thought: Rules—there have to be rules to this game. You can't just overwhelm the contestant with money. That would be cheating. Carefully, he pocketed the wad in his hand and peeled of a twenty. He handed it over. She looked surprised.

"*Senor?*"

"I'd like more towels. Can you bring me towels to Room 1224?" He helped her understand by pointing up.

Maria rattled off a couple of sentences in Spanish, then added, "No my floor. I call maid."

Jason shook his head. "No. I want you. Please. *Por favor.*"

She nodded and said in halting English that she'd be up soon. He went up the elevator, whistling to himself. In his room, he took a quick shower and donned his robe. He stuffed some cash into the pockets. When the knock came at his door, he combed his hair back and went to answer it. Maria was standing there, holding a stack of towels. She looked surprised when she saw that he was already done with his shower.

"*Lo siento, senor.* I hurry."

"It's okay. Come in." He stepped aside and she passed him. She placed the towels on a chair and started to leave, but Jason stopped her.

"No, come here. I want to talk to you."

Maria approached nervously, obviously wary of this strange *gringo.* "*Si?*"

"I'm Mr. Reynolds." He didn't want her to think of him as "Jason" to keep her in a subservient position.

Maria nodded. "*Hola.*"

"How long have you been in U.S.?"

She frowned and for a moment Jason didn't think she would answer. But her training that the guests were always right apparently kicked in and she said, "*Un año.*" One year.

"Do you watch game shows, Maria?"

"*Que?*"

"You know, Price is Right, Jeopardy, Wheel of Fortune?"

Her face lit up. "Oh, *si*! Wheel of Fortune! Very good!"

"Good! I would like to play a game with you, okay? You can win money." He held up some of his cash that he had secreted in his pocket.

She was immediately suspicious. "Oh, no, *senor*. I go."

"Maria," he said and she stopped. "How much money do you make in a day? *Quantos dólars?*"

She hesitated, looking up at his face as if trying to understand why he was asking all these questions. She shrugged. "*Cincuenta dollars.*"

Wow, he thought. She works all day for fifty lousy dollars? This might be easier than he thought.

"In my game, you can earn hundreds of dollars."

She backed up, shaking her head. "I good girl."

"Of course you are!" he said at once. "It's just a game, like Wheel of Fortune! Look," he added, "there are rules and everything." He paused, recalling his limited high school Spanish. "Oh! *Reglamentos!* I stay here, *comprende?* That's rule one." He climbed on the bed and leaned against the headboard, pillows propping him up. "See?"

"And rule two," he held up two fingers, "...is that I can't touch you."

Her eyebrows furrowed. "*Toque?* No touch?"

"No touch."

She stood there, staring. "What I do? In game?"

He smiled. She was going to play now, he knew it.

"I offer you cash for items. For example," he said, pointing to the towels. "I'll give you twenty dollars for the towels."

"*Pero senor*! You no pay! Hotel give."

"I know! That's what makes the game fun!" He held up a twenty and she came forward slowly to take it from his hands. She retreated at once, clearly afraid he might grab her. But he made no effort to move toward her.

"See? No touch! Isn't this fun? You've already earned almost as much as you make in a day!"

Maria nodded and watched him warily.

Jason wanted to see if he could convince her to start giving up items of her clothing next—for that was the real purpose of his game—to corrupt an innocent girl. Why? Just to see if he could. "Okay, I give you ten dollars for your nametag."

She looked down, alarmed. "No! I need! Boss *muy enojoso*. How you say, anger?"

"No, no! The game rules, uh, *reglamentos*, say you get everything back when you leave room. Only for here, okay?"

She nodded slowly. He held up the tenner and she unpinned her nametag and put it on the edge of his bed and leaned forward to take the money. She pointed to the nametag. "I take back, okay?"

He tipped his head. "*Sí*. Later."

The next phase would be harder for there was no easy way to do it. And to follow his own rules, he couldn't just toss a bunch of money at her. No, he would have to offer just enough and not more and maybe go up in increments from there.

"Next part of game. For one hundred dollars, I buy your dress."

Maria recoiled as if she had been shot. "No!"

"Just for a few minutes," he said. "And I can't leave bed!"

"No! No!" She backed up toward the door.

"Two hundred," he said, adding another bill to the one in his hand.

She stopped, her hand on the knob.

"What could you do with two hundred dollars? That's four days' work, isn't it? *Quatro dias trabajo?*"

She nodded. Her face reflected the turmoil going on her mind. Finally she said, "You stay? On bed?"

He nodded. "Part of the rules. I stay."

"No touch?"

"No touch."

She returned, her eyes hungrily on the money. Stepping forward, she tried to grab it from his hand. He jerked it back out of reach.

"No, dress first..." he pointed, "on the end of the bed there. Then the money."

Visibly nervous, Maria hemmed and hawed. Jason remained passively on the bed, waiting. He wasn't about to ruin things now by demanding she decide immediately. After a half-minute, her hands went behind her and found the zipper. He heard the noise of it coming down and tried to keep the elation out of his face. It was working!

He suddenly realized he was having more fun now than he ever had at any bar, tossing around money for overpriced champagne to impress the girls.

The dress parted and Maria shrugged it off her shoulders. She stepped out of it quickly and brought it against her body to cover her bra. She stared at him, her eyes questioning if she could trust him. Of course she couldn't, but she could trust him to obey his own self-imposed rules. He would never leave the bed. And he'd never grab her. He knew if he did, it would ruin everything.

Eventually, Maria allowed the dress to slip away, exposing her plain cotton bra and half-slip to his gaze. She stepped forward and draped it over the end of the bed within easy reach. He could imagine her thinking how quickly she might snatch it up and flee.

He held up the two hundred and she came forward, wary as a cat. He made no move to scare her and let the bills slip from his fingers. He leaned back against the pillows.

"Very good. You're doing well, Maria. See, isn't this game easy?"

She nodded, but her eyes remained wary.

Now for the next hurdle. "For fifty dollars, I'd like to buy your half-slip." He pointed.

She looked down at herself, her mind clearly torn. To remove her slip would expose her panties to the man. This she did not want to do, that much was evident. He added to the rules of the game in his head: Nothing wrong with trying to convince her.

"You've already earned, what, two-hundred sixty dollars? And now you could earn more than three hundred! What could you do with three hundred dollars, Maria?"

She didn't answer and he persisted. "Do you live with your parents here?"

She shook her head. *"Mi tia."* Aunt.

"Are your parents still in Mexico?"

She nodded.

"Are you saving up to help them come across the border?"

That was too much English, and face reflected her puzzlement. He tried again. "Parents? *Padre? Madre?* Come here?"

She shook her head. "No. No want to come."

"So you came up here all alone? Wow. You don't have anyone in Mexico you'd like to have join you? In U.S.?"

Maria bit her lip. *"Mi hermana. Lola."*

"Your sister. Is she younger or older?"

"Joven. Dieciseis."

Sixteen, he thought. Man, she's probably every bit as beautiful as Maria here.

"How old are you?"

"Diecinueve."

Nineteen. And here she was, standing before him in her underwear. Jason was thoroughly enjoying his little game. His conscience seemed mollified by the money he was throwing at her. He knew it was far more than she'd ever seen in a day.

"How much does it cost to hire a coyote?"

Her head jerked up. She recognized the term for a human smuggler right away. He wondered if that was her plan all along— to work here until she could bring her sister over.

She looked down at the rug. *"Dos mil."*

For a moment, Jason thought she meant "millions" and realized she was talking about thousand. Two thousand dollars to pay a coyote. It must seem like a fortune to her.

"How much have you saved so far? *Quantos dólars?"*

Maria stared at him, trying to decide if she should say. "*Trescientos*," she said finally, her voice soft.

"Three hundred? Heck you could earn a lot more right here today." He held up the fifty. "For your slip."

She only thought about it for a moment before tugging it down quickly. She placed it on the bed by his feet. Jason got his first good look at her body now—she had beautiful copper skin and all the right curves. Her panties were the old "granny" type and were not flattering in the least. But her stockings were interesting. They were thigh-high, with elastic tops that gripped her legs. Maybe they were cheaper to buy than panty hose, he mused. But they did give her a sexy look. If she wore smaller briefs, she'd look like a hooker, not a maid.

She was trying to hide herself and he said, "No, no—you must let me look. That's part of the game."

Maria dropped her hands and stood there, her face flushed red. She looked at the ceiling, the floor and everywhere but his face.

He pointed. "Those panties..." he remembered a phrase he'd learned from a high school buddy, "*cosa fea*." Ugly thing.

She blushed a deeper red and turned away.

"You have better panties. *Bonita* panties?

Reluctantly, she nodded. "No for work."

"Well, I hope you'll wear them for me next time." He held up the fifty. "Come and get it."

She lunged forward and snatched it away, then retreated to her place by the chair. She tucked the bill with the others into her bra. He could tell from the way she was jerking her legs, she was nearly at her limit. He wondered if she could be enticed to go a little further.

He fished out another fifty and held it up. Her eyes grew wide and her expression clearly said, Please, no more! But she didn't speak and she didn't gather up her clothes to leave.

"Fifty dollars for your bra."

Maria began shaking her head, back and forth firmly. "No, *senor*. I no play no more." She reached for her clothes.

"Wait."

She stopped and glanced up at him. He tucked the fifty away and pulled out a one-hundred dollar bill. "One hundred." He paused, then went in for the kill. "Think of it. You could walk out of here almost half-way to your goal of two thousand dollars."

She didn't seem to quite comprehend. He pointed to her. "Good money, no?"

She stared at him. "I good girl."

"And you're a very good sister, too, I'll bet. Does Lola write you and ask when she can come up to live with you?"

For the first time, Jason saw tears in Maria's eyes and he felt just a twinge of remorse. *But I'm helping her,* he told himself.

She continued to stare at him. He didn't move, playing the game by his rules. Finally, she said, "You no move?"

Hah! His mind shouted and he fought to keep his expression neutral. "No move. Rules of game," he said.

She stood erect and her hands went behind her back. Her bra slipped loose and her fingers captured the money as her bra fell down her arms and onto the floor. Her hands, full of cash, immediately covered up her breasts.

Jason tsked and shook his head. "No good. You must let me see. Part of game."

Her hands came away now and he got a good look at her lovely breasts. They were young and perky and just about perfect. A C-cup, he guessed, with her nipples already hard in the cool air. Or maybe she's turned on, he mused.

"Turn back and forth." He motioned with his hands and she obliged, moving her body to one side then the other, giving him a wonderful view. He could feel his cock harden in his robe and watched her eyes to see if she noticed.

She stuffed the bills into one hand and came forward to collect the money with the other, covering her breasts with her forearm as she drew near. He held the money out of reach. "Uh huh. You must let me see all the time while we're playing the game."

She lowered her arm and close up, her breasts were even more magnificent. Round and firm and enticing. Jason's lips ached to kiss her erect nipples. Her gaze dropped and he knew she saw his erection tenting his robe. She grabbed at the bills. He let the money slip from his fingers and she retreated back to her post, her upper chest and face mottled with embarrassment. She busied herself by straightening out the wad of bills in her hands.

"You're doing very well, Maria. Would you like to play some more?"

She shook her head. "No, no! I must go!" She pointed to her clothes. "Okay?"

"Wait. I haven't seen enough yet."

He made her stand there, red with shame, while he stared at her naked chest. Finally, he nodded and she quickly started to dress. "If you'd like to play more, come by here tomorrow. What time do you get off of work?"

"Uh, five. No, I no play no more."

"Up to you. But you could have Lola coming here next week, not next year. Think about that, okay?"

She had her clothes back on now and was zipping her dress. *"Si,"* she nodded, clearly eager to be away from there. She picked up her nametag. *"Adios. Gracias."* She left, clutching her wad of bills in her hand.

Jason sat back and laughed, feeling both wicked and generous. It was a heady combination. He thought about calling up an escort service but decided against it. *No, I'll save myself for Maria.*

Maria stepped out into the corridor, her body shaking. *Dios mia!* These crazy rich Americans! She kept the wad of cash tucked inside the pocket of her uniform while she waited for the elevator, her hands fumbling to pin on her nametag. As soon as the elevator doors closed behind her, she yanked out the money and counted it again. Four-hundred-ten dollars! So much money! More than she had seen at one time ever! It was a fortune by her standards and for the first time, Maria had hope that she might see her sister this year instead of in two or three years, as she had expected.

She arrived at the eighth floor and quickly stuffed the money back into her dress. For the rest of her shift, her mind whirled with excitement. When her conscience told her she shouldn't be doing such terrible things in that rich man's bedroom, she told herself: *I'm doing it for Lola.*

CHAPTER TWO

The tentative knock came at his door at ten after five the next day. Jason had made sure he was back in his room by four-thirty and had freshly showered. Like yesterday, he was naked under his robe. All part of his costume for "The Game." Hearing the knock, he grinned widely and whispered to himself: "And returning today, our contestant from Mexico, the lovely Maria!"

He opened the door and Maria was there, dressed in her ugly maid's outfit. He waved her inside and she passed by him. He could tell she was very nervous.

"Hey, relax," he said, closing the door. "This game is fun, no?"

She tipped her head. He knew she meant, *No, it's not fun, but the money's good.*

"Are you ready to play more?"

She took a deep breath and nodded.

"How much did you make yesterday?"

"*Cuatrocientos,*" she said.

He already knew that, of course. He just wanted to remind her how lucrative his game was. He nodded and asked, "And how long did it take you to save three hundred on your own?"

She stared at the floor. "*Un año.*"

He let that sink in before he gave her the bad news. "Well, fine. I'm happy to play with you. But we have to pick up the game where we left off."

She looked up, confused.

"Start game, same place as yesterday," he said. "Remove clothes, we begin."

Her mouth dropped open. No doubt she had imagined that he would buy her clothes all over again, allowing her to reap some cash without losing too much of her modesty. Suddenly, she was faced with the prospect of starting out wearing nothing but panties and stockings. Her head began to shake.

"No! We start new game!"

"No, that's not how it works." He went over and climbed onto the bed. He pulled out a hundred-dollar bill and waved it around. "I'll tell you what, though. If you are wearing sexy panties today, I'll give you a one-hundred-dollar bonus when you strip down to where you were yesterday."

Maria stood there, staring at him. Jason could see the wheels turning in her head. Should she or shouldn't she? It all depended upon which perspective she chose. Which was worse for her, he thought, having Lola stuck in Mexico or giving up a bit of her dignity?

Finally her hands went to her dress and she shrugged out of it, more quickly than last time, and dropped it on the chair next to her. Her slip came next, and Jason could see she had worn a much sexier pair of panties, a light blue lacy number that hugged her slim hips.

He pointed. "You wear those for me?"

She blushed and he felt his cock rise again. God this woman was hot!

"Now the bra," he reminded her.

She shrugged out of it and placed it on the chair. She stood there, visibly shaking.

"Relax, it's okay. You're safe. We follow rules, right?" He held up the bill and she came forward to grab it. He made sure he didn't move. She was skittish enough already.

"Now," he said when she was back into position. "We start game from here. I give you fifty dollars for those cute panties."

Maria shook her head. "No."

"Ohh, are we getting greedy?"

She blushed again but she stood her ground.

18

"Very well, I'll give you fifty dollars for those stockings."

She looked down at them. From Jason's point of view, they appeared to be the same one she had on yesterday. She probably couldn't afford many new things, not on a maid's salary.

Maria shook her head again. *"Más."*

Jason felt disappointment rise for the first time. She was becoming a "dollar belle" right before his eyes. But he told himself he set up the rules, it was no wonder she was trying to squeeze him for all she could get.

"One hundred for the stockings. Final offer."

She opened her mouth to protest and closed it at once. Finally, she nodded and sat on the chair and stripped off her stockings. She stood again, dressed now only in her lacy panties. He made her turn around so he could see everything. She was a beautiful girl. Many hearts were probably broken when she fled to the U.S.

"Okay, now the panties." He held up two fifties. "One hundred dollars."

She shook her head. "No."

Jason debated. Truth be told, he'd pay her five hundred for a look at her cute young pussy. But he promised himself he'd play by the rules and by god, he was going to. He shook his head. "You're getting greedy."

She didn't understand greedy and he couldn't think of the Spanish word. "Uh, you ask for too much."

She stared at him and shrugged. "I go now." She turned toward her clothes.

"Wait."

Maria paused.

He replaced one of the fifties with a hundred dollar bill. "One fifty, that's my final offer."

She stood erect and they stared at each other like gunslingers. He held the money up. At last, she hooked her thumbs into the waistband of her panties and paused, her eyes boring into his.

"You stay? On bed?"

He nodded. "I stay."

She let the panties flutter down to the rug and stepped out of them. Her hands went in front to cover her, but before he could object, she moved them to her sides, giving him a clear view of the dark triangle of soft hair.

"Very nice. Open your legs a little."

This command she understood. She bit her lip and her body shook. But her legs came apart. He peered, trying to see, but her hair covered her up. He got just the barest hint of the incurring line of her pussy. It was a bit of a disappointment.

"Money now?"

"Wait. Come closer. One step."

She hesitated, and moved forward. Her eyes were on the bills in his hand.

"Please. I go."

"Not yet. I want to get my money's worth."

So far, he had paid her three-fifty and he was hoping to prolong the game a little longer. He had a special request for her next and he knew she'd object. He thought about it while Maria wiggled nervously in front of him.

"I can't see anything," he said.

She looked down. "So? I do what you ask."

"Yes, but your hair is too thick down there, I can't see you."

Her dark eyes flashed. "You cheat me?"

"No," he said, holding out the bills. "A deal's a deal. But now I want to offer you another one-fifty if you'll shave your pussy— uh, vagina." He wasn't sure what the word was in Spanish, but her expression told him she understood.

She snatched the bills from his hand and her mouth dropped open in shock. "You very bad man!" She retreated to her clothes and grabbed them up, holding them in front of her.

"Wait. I didn't get my money's worth yet."

"I no care! I leave you!"

"Okay, two hundred dollars."

Maria was still shaking her head as she dropped her clothes and picked up her panties from the floor. She yanked them on.

"Two-fifty."

"What kind of man you are, asking this?" She sputtered, pulling her bra into place.

"Don't girls shave in Mexico?"

"No!"

"But they do here in the U.S.—surely you must know that."

She slowed her angry dressing and tipped her head in acknowledgement. "*Si*. I know. Not me. It is against God."

"Oh, so then you don't shave your armpits, either?"

She stopped now, her panties and bra on but nothing else. "*Si*, I shave there. It is okay."

"Why is that okay with God but not the rest? How about your legs, do you shave them too?"

Maria pursed her lips. "*Si*. Hotel ask us. Say *Americanos* like."

"Well, then. Your argument doesn't hold up. It's not against God—it's against your tradition."

She shrugged. "Maybe. I no do."

"Not even for three hundred?"

That got her attention. He saw tears in her eyes again as the greed began to overcome her willpower. "Why you pay so much?"

"Because I want to help you," he said softly. "I want your sister to come up to live with you and your aunt. She would never have to know how you paid for it."

She hovered there between her morals and her needs. He lay on the bed and tried to keep his expression neutral.

"You no see one before?"

"Not yours. And I'm willing to pay you three hundred to see it naked." He pushed her a little bit more. "You already have three-fifty—you could walk out of here with almost twice that. With the money you've already made, you're just about all the way to your goal!"

Maria gave a long, slow sigh and sat down on the chair. "No trick?"

"No trick."

"You stay, no touch?"

He spread his hands out. "Rules of game."

Finally, she nodded and said, "How I...?"

"First, take off those clothes, then go into the bathroom," he pointed, "and bring out a hot, wet washcloth, a towel, my razor..."

By her expression, she was lost. "Razor." He mimicked shaving his face.

She brightened. "Oh! *Maquinilla de afeitar!*"

"Sounds good. And bring the small can of shaving cream. Oh, and bring out a glass of hot water, too."

She rose reluctantly and stripped off her clothes. He watched as she trudged to the bathroom to fetch the supplies. Jason almost felt sorry for her then. Almost. But it simply proved his point. That all these regular people out there, the ones who considered themselves upright and moral and superior to wastrels like him were nothing more than whores themselves. And he enjoyed proving it.

Maria came back with the equipment gathered in her arms and stood there, uncertainly. He pointed to the other bed next to his.

"Set up there, close by so I can see you."

She moved past him and dumped the items, but she still held the glass of warm water, uncertain where to place it so it wouldn't spill. Finally, she had to step up near Jason and put the glass on the nightstand between the beds. This brought her too close to him for her comfort. Her hands fluttered up to cover her privates.

"Uh uh. You have to let me see."

"You no touch?"

He sighed. This was getting tiresome. "That's the rules. I stay here, I no touch."

She laid the towel out and sat on it, spreading her legs for him. Now he had a much better view of her sweet pussy and knew it was only a matter of time until he was thrusting his hard cock into her. This was going so well! And he hadn't had a drop to drink, either!

She used the wet washcloth to dampen her hair and squirted some shaving cream onto her fingers. She began to daub it on her dark hair and soon had a comic whitish triangle above the fold of skin. Taking the razor and dipping it into the glass, Maria began shaving her hair just for him.

Jason watched, fascinated, his cock hard. He ached to take it out and, while that didn't seem to violate any of his rules, he knew she'd probably panic. So he kept himself still as she slowly shaved, staring at the top and working down, stopping now and then to rinse off the razor in the glass. When the triangle was gone, Jason made her spread her legs wider and get the hairs on both sides of her labia, which she did with great reluctance. But she did it. Soon, her sweet pussy was bare to his eyes.

She tried to jump up, but he stayed her with a word and he stared at her beauty until she flushed a deep red over her copper skin.

"*Por favor, senor,*" she begged.

"Not yet. I want to get my money's worth."

He made her stand up. Now she was within two feet of his gaze. Her body trembled and Jason guessed she feared he would lunge at her. But that would be rape, not to mention a violation of his rules. This game was too much fun to ruin it that way. No, everything she would do would be of her own volition, her own greed.

"Okay," he said at last and she jumped toward her clothes.

"Don't you want to earn any other money today?"

She looked over her shoulder at him. "*Que?* What you want? You see everything."

"Don't you ever masturbate, when you're home alone?"

She apparently knew the word, for she stared at him, shocked. "*Que?*"

"You know, rub yourself?"

"No! I good girl!"

It was hard to keep from laughing at Maria, who still considered herself good although she was standing in a strange man's room, naked and shaved.

"Really? Okay. How about this instead: I give you one-hundred dollars to rub your breasts over my body. Oh, and," he added quickly before she could object, "and I'll impose a new rule on myself." He reached behind him and grabbed the railings of his headboard. "I can't release my hands. So I can't touch you."

She stared at him for a long time. Finally it dawned on her. "You turn me into *puta*!"

Though his Spanish was limited, Jason recognized the word for "whore" immediately. "No, no," he said, trying to placate her even though she was right, "I'm just helping you reach your goal. No one will ever know. I certainly won't tell."

Maria shook her head. "I go now."

"Two hundred. Just for rubbing your breasts over my body for one minute. Think of it—how long would it take you, cleaning rooms, to make that much money?"

She stubbornly shook her head. But Jason noted that she wasn't getting dressed. He pushed her a little further. "Two-fifty. That's my final offer."

She slowly turned around. "One minute? You no hurt me?"

"No. See?" His hands firmly gripped the railing over his head.

She stepped forward. Her body was achingly beautiful and his cock was at full attention. Maria came to his bed and hesitated there. She leaned down and rubbed her left breast against the robe over his thigh.

"Oh, no," he said. "You have to unfasten the robe first. I have to be naked or it's no go."

She straightened up. "*Desnudo?* No!"

"Hey, you're naked, I want to be naked too."

Maria studied him for a long moment. "*Trescientos*," she said, her eyes narrowing.

He gave it a few minutes so she could see how hard he was thinking about it. But he would've done it for five hundred! Finally he said, "Okay, three hundred—but for two minutes, not one." He looked at the clock. "That's until five-fifty-two."

Maria nodded, then leaned forward to unfasten his sash and part his robe. His cock sprang up and startled her. Taking a deep breath, she began to rub her breasts over his body, climbing up on the bed to cover all of his exposed skin. Her ponytail fell over her shoulder, tickling his flesh and adding to his pleasure.

Jason groaned. He was in heaven. He lay there as this cute young woman rubbed her breasts all over, trying to spend the least amount of time on his cock. But he noted that she didn't ignore his erection. He watched as her mouth came open and she began to breathe more heavily. This was turning her on! In just two short days, he had turned this innocent maid into a whore, doing very sexy acts for money. Now for the last part, he thought. He glanced at the clock—the two minutes were up.

"I'll give you another one hundred if you make me come." He tried to think of the equivalent word in Spanish. "Uh, orgasm?"

She recognized that word immediately. She pulled back, just as he expected she would. "No," she said. But her voice lacked conviction and her face appeared flushed. She was definitely aroused, he noted. Her nipples were hard points on her breasts.

"One hundred if you use your hand and three hundred if you use your mouth."

"No, no," she said, shaking her head, staring at his cock. Her mind was reeling with the amount of money she already had—she couldn't even add it all up in her head! And now he was offering more if she'd just help him come. Maria knew all about men's wicked desires—back home, she had masturbated her boyfriend Luis a few times. He had wanted to do a lot more, of course, but she had been able to keep him satisfied with handjobs and letting him stroke her breasts. But she had never kissed any man's *pene*!

She couldn't deny that she'd been tempted during those times when Luis had aroused her. Just looking at his hard cock had made her want to stop being a good girl and allow these naughty feelings to take over. But she'd been strong—her mother had raised a good daughter.

"No, no!" she had said whenever Luis tried to reach into her jeans. *"Nosotros esperan!"* We wait!

Now things seemed to have changed. Her new life in the U.S. had turned everything upside down. All she did was work, eat and sleep. Luis had been unable to afford the journey to the United States, and Maria had felt lonely ever since she had arrived. That didn't excuse what she was doing with this crazy man, but she could understand temptation. And her mother was nowhere near. Her Aunt Consuela tried to be a good substitute but she worked just as hard as Maria, saving to bring her own family over the border.

As she stared at this *gringo's* cock, a voice in her head said, "You can earn the money you need and no one will know." If that wasn't bad enough, another voice, more powerful and visceral, said, "Do it because you want to."

She could feel it in her breasts, stomach and loins. This rich American was exciting her, making her think wicked thoughts.

No one will know!

"Come on, you know you want to. It will be our secret," Jason said.

Maria licked her lips.

"Have you ever kissed a man's cock before?"

She shook her head.

"I can teach you how to do it. All girls should learn, don't you think?"

Maria hesitated, but her eyes never left his erection.

"Just kiss it, right near the tip. I'll bet you've never tasted one before, have you?"

She bit her lip and Jason saw she was beginning to bend down. In slow motion, she moved down until her lips were just inches away from his straining cock. She closed the gap and gave the mushroom head the barest kiss.

"No, harder," he said.

She kissed it again, more firmly, using the tip of her tongue to taste it. Since he was freshly washed, he figured he would not offend her. Suddenly, something within her seemed to take over and she enveloped the tip, using her tongue to swirl around the head.

"Ohhhh," he groaned. "That's so good. You're doing great. Now just ease down over it a bit more."

And just like that, Maria the "good girl" began giving Jason a blowjob. As hummers go, hers wasn't very accomplished. She used too much saliva and gagged repeatedly although she never went further than half-way down his shaft. But it was glorious, just the same. He had her now. It was only a matter of pushing her to the next step.

Although it was very arousing, he couldn't quite come so he told her to use her hand on his shaft. Her hand reached out and grabbed him eagerly, he noticed. She seemed to be enjoying this now. Her hand pumped as she noisily sucked at his cock. Jason began offering directions, making her do it just right and soon felt his seed rising.

"Good, good, ohhh, it's happening!"

She pulled back and he squirted a load of semen all over her face. She recoiled as if she'd been shot and sat up, coughing.

"Ohhhh," he moaned, so happy to have finally come after two days of foreplay.

Maria ran into the bathroom and didn't come out for ten minutes. When she did, her face was flushed and her eyes wild. She stared at his flaccid cock. Then she headed for her clothes.

"Wait. Let me help you."

She turned. "Help me? Oh. *Seiscientos.*" Maria came forward, her hand outstretched.

He found the six hundred in bills in his pocket and passed them over. "No, I mean, let me help you come. Uh, orgasm?"

She shook her head. "No, no."

"Come on, aren't you on edge? Don't you want to?"

"Not right. God not like."

"Sure he does. Otherwise, he would've have given us the ability to come without fucking."

It was the first time he had used that work and she seemed embarrassed by it. Clearly she knew what it meant. He wondered what the teenagers called it in Mexico.

"Maria, you helped me and now I want to help you. Look at you—you're so tense!"

She nodded. "I bad girl." More tears flowed down her cheeks. But again, Jason noted she did not put on her clothes. He opened his arms. "I promise to use my fingers only. You know you're so frustrated now you can hardly stand it."

He expected her to flee but she surprised him. She came into his arms and he put them around her. It was the first time he had touched her and she no longer acted like he was a big bad rapist. His left hand rubbed her bare breast while his right snaked around her waist to rest on her bare mound. She was still skittish and she shivered in his embrace.

"No fuck. Okay?"

So she did know the American idiom. "Sure, okay. Just touching. That's all."

Maria nodded and he began to stroke her skin gently. His hand snuck down to her opening and he felt the wetness there. Her legs moved apart a little to give him better access. He began to slide his fingers up and down, coating them generously, before he brought them up to find her tiny marble of flesh that represented the core of her. With his other hand, he brushed her nipple, feeling it extend out in anticipation. He had to change position so he could bend down and suck on it gently. He moved his left hand into place between her legs and kept rubbing her clit. Maria began to moan.

He moved his mouth to her other nipple and sucked at it. His fingers slipped inside her and he felt her hymen right away. She seemed alarmed and pushed at his hand. He immediately pulled it out and concentrated on her clit. She settled down. In a moment, Jason felt her hand on his cock, which was starting to rise again. She squeezed it gently, pleasing him.

Maria threw her head back against his shoulder and began muttering in Spanish. Jason smiled and increased his speed and pressure. Her body was shaking now and she was close. He nipped at her nipple and that sent her over the edge. She tensed up suddenly and cried out, sweat suddenly appearing on her smooth body.

"*Dios mio!*" she cried out and climaxed, her body jerking in his arms.

He held her tight until she came down. Then she realized she was still holding on to his hard cock and released it and began to cry softly.

"Shhh," he said, comforting her. "Don't feel bad. It's natural. You are a beautiful girl."

"I *puta!*" she blubbered.

"No you aren't! What we did was innocent!"

She snuffled against his shoulder, her naked body pressed to him. He wanted to fuck her so bad he couldn't stand it, but he would have to overcome this last barrier carefully. He wasn't about to rape her. He wanted this to be her idea.

"I must go," she said.

"Just rest for a minute. Enjoy the feeling. There's no rush."

They cuddled there for a few minutes until Maria stopped crying. He leaned over and kissed her on the cheek. She turned and smiled at him and he kissed her gently on the lips. "You like me?" she asked, like an innocent school girl.

"Yes, of course I do. I liked you from the first moment I saw you from the elevator."

She nodded remembering it. She gave a little giggle. "You go up and come right back down!"

He laughed. "Yes I did. You captivated me."

A frown stole across her face. "Then why you pay so much money?"

"I figured you could use it. And I really liked playing the game."

Maria looked deep into his eyes. "You play game with anyone else?"

"Oh? Are you jealous?"

She shrugged.

"No, no one else."

His hand moved back to her wetness and stroked her there. She started to object but he didn't stop and soon he could see in her eyes

29

that she was on the way to another orgasm. He kissed her breasts and rubbed her skin and was pleased to feel her hand return to his cock and encircle it.

He teased her until she was on the verge of coming, then moved his hand away and pushed her down, positioning his body between her legs. She pressed her hands against his chest in alarm, saying. "No! No fuck!"

Jason leaned over to the nightstand and opened the drawer. He pulled out a condom and held it up for her to see, then ripped it open with his teeth. "No worries. You're safe," he said.

"No! I virgin!" She struggled underneath him.

"How about another five hundred?"

She stopped moving and just stared at him, her mouth open. She seemed incapable of speech. There was no question what she was now.

Jason quickly unrolled the condom over his cock. She just watched and bit her lower lip. He positioned his thighs against hers and pushed her wide open, then aimed his cock at her slippery opening and thrust forward. He felt the tearing and watched as Maria's eyes went wide and her mouth opened in a silent scream.

She tried to stop him now but it was too late. Jason pulled back and thrust again. And again, until her expression turned into something beyond shock. He kept thrusting deep within her and finally she grabbed onto him and hung on, her mouth still open but her eyes glazing into a pleasure she had never before experienced.

"*Dios mio!*" she whispered as she hung on tight. Her hips began to move with his and he could hear her voice climbing toward her release. Jason hung on, trying to match his climax with hers until they reached the peak together and she squealed and he came inside her, feeling her sweet pussy clutching at his throbbing cock.

He held her in his tight grip until his muscles began to relax and he felt suddenly sleepy. He would've liked to take a short nap but Maria was already feeling recriminations.

"*Bastardo!*" She tried to push him off. He was too heavy and his cock was still firmly impaled in her newly fucked pussy.

"Shhh," he said. "Wait a minute. Wait a minute."

"You ruin me! No man want me now!" She began to cry all over again.

"I want you," he said.

She paused. "You want me?"

"Yes. Very much. I want to see you every day after work. Okay?"

She thought about that. "But we no, uh, *amantes*! You just fucker."

He didn't know what *amantes* meant, but he could guess. Jason had really no intention of starting up a relationship and just considered this part of his game. He'd be gone in a few days anyway. By that time, Maria would be well paid and well fucked.

"But I really like you, Maria."

Her innocent face grew hopeful. "But you rich man. I poor."

"That doesn't really matter, does it?"

"But you pay me! For sex!"

"I paid you for the game. Do you want me to stop paying you now?"

He could see she started to say yes and then her greed took over. "If you want to, it okay."

"Good." He felt his cock stiffen inside her. He had no sperm left, but he liked having this control over her. He moved his cock and her eyes opened wide.

"More?" she whispered.

"More," he said.

As she rode the bus home, Maria tried not to think about what had happened. Her mind screamed at her and she could only protect herself by blocking out images of Mr. Reynolds' naked body looming over her or the feeling of her hymen tearing as he thrust into her. She had given up her precious gift for a few dollars. Okay, a lot of dollars. Even now the wad of cash felt like a lead weight in her pocket. She hadn't even counted it.

Her pussy felt wet and violated. No man would want her. She'd grow up like her Aunt Consuela, lonely and desperate for the affections of a good man. Consuela was just thirty-five, yet already her hard life had coarsened her. When she had come across the border twelve years ago, she had been young and pretty and full of hope, just like Maria. Her letters had always seemed so cheerful. When Maria first joined her, she was shocked at the change in her. Now Aunt Consuela seemed resigned to working hard for little money and had no man to cook for or to share her bed.

Consuela had never talked about what had happened to her, only that "she never met the right man." Did she give up her virginity to a rich American too? She could never ask, for that would be rude. But it might explain her sadness. A sadness she now shared.

I do it for you, Lola, she thought, but it failed to cheer her up.

Her aunt was at work when she got back to the small apartment. Maria stripped off her clothes and took a long shower in the tepid water, trying to wash off the smell of Mr. Reynolds. Only later, when she had dressed in jeans and a T-shirt, did she sit down and count her ill-gotten gains. Blood money, she thought ruefully. Virgin blood.

Seven-hundred fifty dollars, including the extra five hundred dollars he had given her after he had raped her. No, it wasn't a rape, was it? She had accepted his money. The memory of it burned, for it made her a whore. All together, she had more than the two thousand she needed. Her mind was jumbled with thoughts. She knew she shouldn't return to Mr. Reynolds' room, and yet, why not? She was already a fallen woman. What more could he do to her? And she and Lola could use the money.

CHAPTER THREE

The next day at five, Jason began training Maria to be his whore. He had to be careful, for she probably still had innocent imaginings of them going off into the sunset together. If he pushed too far, too fast, she'd wake up from her silly visions and be distraught.

When the knock came, Jason was still dressed. He invited her in and immediately made her strip off all her clothes. He didn't offer to pay her and she hesitated only for a moment before complying. He loved watching the clothes fall from her nubile body. Her nipples were hard and she had that blush of embarrassment. When she was naked, he told her to drop to her knees and practice sucking his cock.

She seemed shocked by his demeanor and he softened it at once.

"Remember, I'm trying to teach you to be a good lover for me. Don't you want to please me?"

Maria seemed a bit confused by everything, but she went along. In her eyes, Jason thought he could see the greed there, and could guess that she was wondering when he would offer to pay her. But couples don't pay each other, do they? He let her think what she wanted.

She unzipped him and took his hard cock into her mouth. He instructed her on how to do it, pressing her to take more into her mouth. "You want to do this the way I like it, don't you?" he said. She nodded around his cock.

He made her continue until he felt he was ready to come. He pulled her to her feet and bent her over the bed. She lay there, her ass up and looked over her shoulder at him, confusion on her face. He pulled a condom out of his pocket and slipped it on.

"So fast?" she said.

He nodded and pressed his cock inside her. He hadn't even bothered to get undressed. He fucked her hard and fast and when he came, he could tell she had not climaxed. He pulled out and yanked the condom off and tossed it into the trash. Only then did he get undressed, watching Maria who lay there breathlessly.

They climbed into bed under the covers and he cuddled with her. This was also an important step, for it reinforced both his need for rough, quick sex and his alleged caring for her. They nestled together while he told her how much she meant to him. He never used the word "love," however.

When Jason felt himself grow hard once again, he rolled her over onto her back and thrust into her all at once before she could object. Her eyes went wide and she cried out, "No! You make baby!"

He ignored her and fucked her quickly once more, driving her to a climax despite her fears. He didn't want to complicate things with a pregnancy either, so just before he came, he pulled out and squirted onto her belly. She seemed enormously grateful and hugged him close.

"You have to learn to trust me," he said and she nodded. "Besides, you should go on the pill. I don't like condoms."

She became very quiet. He could imagine her lying there, thinking about what that all meant. Was she his girlfriend now? Would they get married and have babies? Being married to a rich American would be a dream come true. Jason didn't dissuade her from her fantasy.

Jason doubted he could come again, but to make sure, he pulled back the covers and made Maria go down and suck him again. "You need the practice," he told her.

She made a face when she saw how her own fluids coated his cock, so Jason slapped her ass a couple of times, making her jump.

"Hey! What you do?"

"Girls who don't obey need to be spanked." He spanked her twice more again, just to show he could. She rubbed her ass, but then bent down and took his soft cock into her mouth. Something about her subservience made him hard again and he pushed her down onto the bed and fucked her one last time. This time, he didn't pull out when she came because he had nothing left. However, he did fake his own climax.

Her eyes grew wide. "You came? In me?" She grew pale.

"It's okay—no sperm left. But like I said, I want you to go on the pill. See a doctor tomorrow."

"But I work all day! And I no have doctor."

"Doesn't your aunt have a doctor?"

She looked shocked. "I no tell her! She think I virgin!" Tears came to her eyes.

"If I set it up, will you do it for me?"

She nodded though there was doubt in her eyes.

Good. She was becoming his obedient little slave.

Jason nodded. "All right. I know a guy. Come by here tomorrow at five." In fact, he had set it up already. He knew a "doctor to the stars" who dispensed pills like party favors was in town for a vacation. He had tracked him down that afternoon and offered to trade the prescription for some fun and games, but he cautioned "Dr. Smith"— not his real name, of course—that Maria wouldn't be fully trained for a few more days. He outlined what he had been up to.

Dr. Smith, a tall man with a full head of gray hair that gave him a professional appearance even though he was a reprobate, had loved the idea. He said he'd put her on Lybrel, a new pill that stops periods for months. He warned Jason he'd have to wait two days before she was fully protected.

Maria seemed confused. "Here? Doctor meet me here?"

"He's on vacation here in Miami," he told her. "Don't worry, he's a good doctor."

She nodded. It was time for her to go. As she got dressed, Jason slipped five hundred dollars out of his wallet and handed it to her. She looked down at it as if it was something distasteful, but she accepted it anyway. She dressed quickly and left.

Maria felt terrible and elated at the same time. She had more than enough money! She would write Lola and tell her at once—she will be so happy! But how can she explain her sudden wealth? Lola and her mother might think it was something bad or illegal. And they would be right. She'd have to figure out a way to make it sound innocent or fortuitous.

On the long bus ride home, she wracked her brain trying to come up with a good explanation they would accept. Telling them someone loaned her the money seemed the best idea—he'd have to pretend to pay it back over time. She could say Mr. Reynolds offered the money after he heard her sad story. It might work.

She would have to find Lola a job right away. Perhaps she could work at the hotel with her. Maria would have to ask Esmeralda, the head maid. She knew their jobs were popular among new immigrants for it was easier work than many other jobs. It would be worth asking. If not, Lola could find something here—everyone was so rich!

Once safely in her apartment, Maria pulled the wad of bills from under her mattress and added to the five hundred she received today. She counted it again and again: Two thousand eight hundred and fifty dollars! All in just three days. The loss of her virginity seemed somehow small and petty compared to what she would be able to do with her life now.

Then another thought came to her. Mr. Reynolds wanted to see her again. How much more money could she make? She might make enough to move out and get her own place with Lola! Her stomach flip-flopped as she contemplated selling her body for money. But part of her said: *You've already sold it. What difference does it make now?*

CHAPTER FOUR

D r. Smith was waiting with Jason in his hotel room at five. The doc was sipping a glass of bourbon from a bottle he'd brought along and Jason drank a soda water as they talked about his little experiment.

"You are a very bad man, Jason," the doctor said. "You know you'll burn in hell for this."

"I know. But it was the most fun I've had since I stopped drinking."

"What's going to happen when you leave? Have you thought about what that might do to her?"

"Well, you'll be in town a while longer, won't you? Maybe you could help her out."

The doctor laughed. "Maybe. I'm not sure I need a little whore running around, though. I get plenty of pussy as it is!"

Jason had no doubt—a doctor who was free with his prescription pad was like chocolate to high-strung, beautiful women. All he had to do was show up at the hotel pool and he'd have his pick of ladies who knew his reputation.

"Well, let's worry about that later. I'm sure we can think of something."

A knock came at the door. Dr. Smith hurried into the bathroom and tossed the remains of his drink into the sink and began washing his hands. Jason went to answer the door.

"Hello, Maria! Come in. I have Dr. Smith here. He wants to give you a quick exam and then he can prescribe the pills."

She came in nervously, looking around. Dr. Smith came out of the bathroom, drying his hands on a clean towel.

"Hello, Maria. I'm Dr. Smith."

She nodded, her eyes downcast. Her body began to tremble.

"Please remove your clothes and lie on the bed," the doctor said.

Maria looked from Jason to the doctor and back again.

"It's all right, Maria," Jason said soothingly. "He's a doctor and I've already seen you, right?"

With nervous fingers, she began to strip. The men watched silently as her clothes came off. Today, she was wearing a very sexy bra and bikini panty set—pink with lace, top and bottom. Jason guessed she had gone shopping to buy something nice with her rich boyfriend's money. Good for her, he thought.

When she was dressed only in her bra and panties, she hesitated again, her eyes beseeching Jason to stop her. But he just smiled and nodded. The rest of her clothes came off and she covered herself up.

"Now, please lie on the bed, right here," Dr. Smith told her in a soothing voice.

Maria obeyed, still trying to hide herself as she did. Both men keep their faces kindly and caring but Jason was sure Dr. Smith was thinking: what a beautiful, sexy girl! When she was in position up against the pillows, Dr. Smith placed his little black bag up on the bed and opened it. He took out a stethoscope and held the disk against her chest. He listened to her heart and lungs and told her to cough. Maria relaxed a bit and perhaps thought that was all the doctor needed. If she had only known!

The doctor put the stethoscope away and pulled on a pair of rubber gloves. Maria seemed alarmed. He pushed her back against the pillows and moved her legs apart. Once again she looked up to Jason for help. He just shook his head firmly.

Dr. Smith took out a small flashlight and shined it on her naked cleft. "I see you shave," he said and Maria's face grew bright red.

"Oh, I asked her to do that, doctor," Jason said helpfully. The doctor already knew all about it, of course. They simply enjoyed embarrassing her. "But she's getting a bit stubbly. She'll have to shave again today, I think."

The doctor nodded. "Good. It's much more hygienic that way. Keep it up." He eased two fingers of his right hand into her pussy while keeping the light trained on her with his left. Maria began to jerk back.

"Just slap her bottom if she disobeys," Jason said. "She responds to that."

The doctor chuckled. "Just relax, Maria. I'm just checking your responses here." His fingers slid back and forth. This was no medical procedure, but the doctor was certainly enjoying himself. He moved deeper into her and now she could help but respond. Her breath grew shallow and her eyes seemed to unfocus.

"How long ago did you lose your virginity?" the doctor asked as if this was another routine question that he didn't already know the answer to.

"Uh! Oh!" Her face grew red. *"Ayer.* Uh, yesterday."

Jason saw the tears that sprung from her eyes and actually felt a twinge of regret.

"Oh! I see." He looked over his shoulder at Jason—his hand never stopped working. "Well, Jason's a lucky man to have such a sweet girl."

"Pl-please," she begged, hovering now on the brink of an orgasm and fighting it.

"What?" he asked innocently, his fingers moving faster now.

"Por favor, detener!"

He didn't stop and she could no longer fight it. The dam burst within her as she came in a rush, her head falling back onto the pillows, her body shaking. "OOOOHHH!"

The doctor could see her pussy vibrate wildly and felt it grip his fingers tightly as if to squeeze a load of sperm from them.

"Good," he said, pulling out.

Maria blushed bright red from her stomach to her face, making her cooper skin seem to glow. She put a hand over her eyes.

He snapped off his gloves and threw them in the waste basket. "You are a lucky man, Jason. Her vaginal response is excellent."

"Well, she *is* nineteen," Jason replied, smiling.

They were talking about her as if she wasn't there, naked and spread out, coming down from a powerful orgasm. Maria hid behind her hand.

"I have some sample packs. You can get started right away. I'll need to come back in a couple of days to check on you."

Maria spoke up, seemingly alarmed. "Doctor, what about my..." She couldn't think of the English word, "...*menstruación?*"

"Oh, don't worry about that. This pill eliminates your periods for as long as you take it." He rummaged through his bag. "I have two sample packs to get you started. And here's a prescription." He jotted something down on a pad and handed it over.

"Now it's important to take the pills at exactly the same time every day."

"How about now?" Jason asked. "I can keep them to make sure."

"Yes, that would work." He popped one out of the package. "Here. I'll get you some water."

Maria looked up at Jason, the pill in her hand and her face a mass of confusion. It was all happening so fast!

Dr. Smith returned with a glass of water and the two men watched as she took the pill. "If you feel any discomfort, you let me know when I return, okay?"

Maria nodded, her eyes wide.

"Good. And Jason, you can't fuck her without a condom for two more days."

She visibly recoiled at the crude talk.

"I won't, doc."

The doctor closed his bag and stood. "I'll be off then. Good luck." When he had turned his back to Maria, he winked at Jason. He saw Dr. Smith to the door and returned to see Maria still lying on the bed, naked, a shocked expression on her face.

"Isn't this great, honey?" he said. "Soon we won't have to worry about those damn condoms."

"He-he made me..."

"What? Come? He had to check your responses, didn't he?"

Her body visibly shook. "I so embarrassed!"

"You've never been to a doctor before?"

"*Si*, but no like him!"

Jason laughed. "Well, it's over now. Come over here and give me a blow job, sweetie." He sat down in the chair. She stared at him for a long time. He added, "Unless you want another spanking…"

She crawled off the bed and came to him, tears flowing from her eyes. She unzipped him and freed his hard cock. Just before she took it into her mouth, she looked up at him and asked, "I just *puta*, no?"

"Oh, no! Not at all! I just really enjoy having you take care of me!" he lied.

She nodded but did not seem convinced. Nevertheless, she bent down and took his cock into her mouth. Maria was getting much better at it now. He needed to make only a few suggestions before he felt the urge to come. He debated. Come in her mouth or use a condom and come in her pussy? He still disliked the condoms and decided to just let go right away. His climax rose until he was gasping. Just before he erupted, he pushed her head down hard on his cock and felt his cock explode into her throat. She coughed and gagged and forced her head up, sucking in a great, shuddering breath, her face pink.

"Mr. Reynolds!" She got up and staggered to the bathroom. Jason could hear her washing out her mouth.

She returned, a towel in one hand. "You scare me."

"I'm so sorry—I was just trying to show you how to swallow correctly. You're not supposed to let it go down the wrong pipe!"

He went to her and enveloped her in his arms. She allowed him the hug, although he could tell she was miffed. After a few minutes of holding her and whispering endearments, she calmed down. He led her to the chair and told her she could get dressed. When she was ready, he counted out two hundred dollars and pressed it into her hand.

She looked up sharply. "Yesterday, it five hundred."

"Yes, but yesterday you sucked and fucked. Today, suck only. Now tomorrow," he continued before she could protest, "I want you to come to my room without panties, okay? In fact, I don't want you to wear panties all day."

Maria's eyes grew wide. "I can't!"

"Sure you can. If you don't, I'll have to spank you." He escorted her to the door, ignoring her sputtering. "Unless you like a little spanking. Some girls do, you know."

"But Mr. Reynolds! What if I no come to your room? What you do then, huh?"

"Oh no, you must come. Or I'll come for you. You wouldn't want to be spanked in some stranger's hotel room, would you? Besides, you have to take your pill, remember? Same time every day or it won't work, that's what the doctor said."

He opened the door and she stepped out, still confused. He smiled. "See you tomorrow, my dear." He closed the door, leaving her standing there bewildered.

Jason waited a half-hour and went downstairs to meet Dr. Smith in the bar. He ordered a club soda while his friend had his bourbon. Just looking at the glass of amber liquid made body ache with need.

"How'd she take it?"

Jason turned his attention away from Smith's glass. "Pretty good. She's showing few signs of resistance."

"You think she'll be ready for me day after tomorrow? I have some GBH, if you need it."

Jason waved a hand. "Oh, no, that would violate the rules of the game. But I hope so. I'll call if you there's a change in plans."

Smith laughed. "You are a weird one, Jason. How did you come up with this idea?"

"It was either that or start drinking again."

He nodded. "I hear ya. I may have to do the rehab myself one day."

Jason finished his club soda. "So tomorrow would be too soon to fuck her, huh?"

"Yeah, probably. Last thing you want is to knock her up, right?"

"Yeah. But she's so tasty—I can hardly keep my hands off of her."

"I'm amazed that you got her so far along so fast. What was it—three days from innocent virgin to cock-sucking whore?"

"Something like that. Just goes to show you what people will do for money."

"You have paid her a lot. You could hire pros for less, I imagine."

Jason nodded. "Sure. But where would be the fun in that?"

He explained what he wanted the doctor to do tomorrow and left. Jason walked downtown to a bookstore and picked up an English-Spanish dictionary. Might come in handy, he mused.

CHAPTER FIVE

At three o'clock the next afternoon, Jason went looking for his little whore. He wanted to see if she had obeyed him. He found her on the eighth floor, cleaning an empty room. He closed the door behind him. She looked up from making the bed, surprise on her face.

"Mr. Reynolds! I not done..."

He didn't say anything, he just ran his hand underneath her dress until he could feel her panties. He shook his head. Maria grew pale.

"But sir! I must wear, um, *mi bragas*! Someone might see!"

Jason still didn't speak. He sat down on the bed and grabbed her, turning her over on his knee. She fought, but not too hard. Soon he had her dress up and her panties down and was spanking her hard on her bare bottom. She squealed and cried but he ignored her. When he was finished and her ass bright red, he dumped her onto the carpet.

"Give them to me," he ordered her.

Whimpering, Maria slid the panties off her legs and handed them over.

"Stand up."

She did, facing him.

"Raise your dress. Spread your legs apart."

She obeyed him, that pretty pink flush spreading again. He bent down and looked at her pussy. She looked everywhere but at his face. He could see she was wet already. She also needed a shave again—her mound was prickly with black stubble.

He reached in and ran his finger along her wetness, watching her face. She closed her eyes and her mouth came open. "Look at you, dying to get off, and yet you can't even obey simple instructions."

"Sorry, sir," she mumbled. Her hips started to jerk. She was close to coming. He stopped. Her eyes flew open.

"That's enough for now. Don't you dare come before you show up to my room at five." He stood, pocketing the panties. "Oh, and Maria?"

"Yes, Mr. Reynolds?"

He pointed. "I want that shaved before you come up."

Her face went white. "But...! How! I no have..." she lapsed into Spanish. Jason could guess she was saying "shaving cream and razor."

"That's your problem. You should've shaved at home. You should remain well shaved at all times."

Her expression was priceless. "You no say! You no say that!"

"Once you shaved for me, you should've known I wanted it kept that way. Your job is to please me, remember?"

He left her there, whimpering, her dress askew, her panties in his pocket. He knew he was pushing her hard, but he had to—the game demanded it. Perhaps that's how he'd measure success—by how long it took the corruption to take place.

Whistling to himself, he went upstairs and put his swim suit on. He grabbed a towel and swam some laps in the hotel pool until four, then retreated to his room to shower and read a book. At five-twenty, the knock came at his door.

He got up and opened it to see Maria standing there. She looked beaten down, like a scared puppy. She started to scoot past him but he blocked her way.

"Well?" he said.

Maria seemed confused. "Sir?"

"Did you shave?"

She nodded.

"Show me."

Her mouth came open. She glanced up and down the corridor. "Don't worry about that. Worry about me. Show me."

With shaking hands, she lifted the front of her pink uniform until her naked mound came into view. She had shaved. He didn't know how she did it, but she had. The elevator dinged and Maria quickly snatched her dress down to cover herself.

"I wasn't done," he said.

She stared at him as a couple walked past. They seemed oblivious to the drama being played out in front of them. They passed on down the hall and Maria's eyes followed them. When they disappeared into a room, she lifted her dress once again.

"Not good enough," he said. "When I say show me, I expect you to do it right away and keep it there until I tell you it's all right to lower it."

"But those people! I get fired!"

"You really worried about that? You really want to keep your crappy job when you've got me?"

Her mouth opened and closed. He guessed she wanted to ask just what that meant, but wasn't sure how to form the right words.

He stepped aside. "Come in, it's time for your pill and your punishment."

She came in, her dress still held up. "Pun-ish?

He grinned. *"Castigo."* He had looked the word up.

Her face registered shock. "But I do what you ask!"

Jason closed the door, but not all the way. She didn't notice. "Yes, you did great job shaving for me. But you lowered your dress before I was done inspecting your sexy pussy."

He liked the effect his words had on her. "Well? Take off your clothes."

More tears flowed but she did as she was told. He held up a pill and a glass of water and she gulped down her medicine. He went to the bed and sat down, patting his lap. She came over meekly and laid herself over his lap, her ass up. She was still a bit pink from her earlier spanking. He spanked her again, harder this time, until she was begging and pleading and speaking rapidly in Spanish. When he finished, his hand hurt. He'd have to use something else next time, he decided.

"Oww! *Me duelen la cula!"*

"Next time, do what you're told. Now let's see how you much you've learned about cock-sucking."

She unzipped his pants and dove quickly on his cock, afraid any delay might result in more punishments. She was getting better, but Jason needed to hold off a few more minutes. He made her stop and practice her technique, learning to deep-throat him. He told her he wanted to come down her throat today and didn't want her to choke and explained how she needed to swallow, not try to breathe in.

He had her start again and when she was really getting into it and he felt he was ready to come, the door was pushed open and Dr. Smith entered. Maria didn't see him at first, as her back was to the door. But she became aware of him when he closed the door behind him and her eyes went wide. She tried to pull up but Jason grabbed her head and thrust her mouth down on his cock, just as he began to squirt into her.

Because she was so startled, she again coughed and hacked, pulling herself up to breathe. She covered her face and breasts with her hands and ran into the bathroom.

"It's only the doctor, Maria," Jason called after her, winking at Smith. "He's come for another exam!"

"Please! I...*mucha verguenza!*"

Jason scanned quickly through his dictionary. "Ah! Embarrassed!"

He turned to the door. "He's a doctor, Maria! Please come out."

The door opened and she peeked around it, taking in the two men.

"It's all right, Maria. Come here, he doesn't have all day. He's seen lots of naked girls before."

She crept out, eyes on the rug.

"Please get on the bed, Maria," the doctor said. She obeyed and he brought his bag up and placed it next to her. Just as he did before, he took out the stethoscope and listened to her heart and lungs. Then he made her spread her legs apart as he probed around her vagina with fingers. This time he put a rubber glove only on his left hand. Maria's eyes beseeched Jason. He ignored her.

When she felt his bare fingers of his right hand sliding apart her pussy, she moaned and turned red. "No right," she mumbled. "No right."

"What was that?" Jason asked.

"Doc make me…" she shuddered, unable to say the word.

"You mean 'come'?" Jason said. "How do they say it in Mexico?" He fetched the dictionary.

"I think the word in Spanish is simply *orgasmo*," Dr. Smith replied, his fingers even now starting to probe deep inside her.

She began to respond, despite her mortification. "Why you do this?" she squeaked, shaking her head.

"I need to test your responses. I thought we went over this before," he said firmly, as if explaining something to a child.

"Ohhhh!"

"Here, Jason, why don't you test this, see if this is what you remembered when your penis was inside her." He pulled his fingers out, leaving Maria on the edge.

Jason came forward and substituted his own fingers and began stroking her just as the doctor had. Maria gasped and seemed ready to come. He pulled out.

"Yes, that seems to be about right. Her pussy really can squeeze a man's cock, that's for sure."

"Good." He replaced his fingers and started anew. Maria was shaking now, her breasts vibrating with her approaching climax. Dr. Smith ran the gloved index finger of his left hand over her sopping wet pussy to coat it, then found the rosebud of her asshole and pressed it in just as she reached her peak.

It was as if he had electrocuted her. She gasped and her head jerked back, the cords of her neck standing taut, then she came so hard, she shook the bed against the wall, once, twice, three times.

"OOOOOOHHHHHHHHH!" she bellowed, writhing on his fingers. Dr. Smith glanced over at Jason and nodded his approval.

"Madre dios!" Maria cried, another spasm shaking her.

When she settled down, the doctor pulled his fingers out of her and announced. "Normal responses. You'll be ready to fuck tomorrow, my dear."

She blanched but she was too weak to protest.

Dr. Smith pulled off his glove and threw it away, stood up and closed his bag. Maria watched him, expecting him to leave. But he did something that stunned her. He came up to the head of the bed and unzipped his pants. He pulled out his hard cock.

Maria looked up at Jason, her eyes wide with shock.

"Come on, Maria, that's his pay for services," Jason said. "It's no big deal."

"Yeah," the doctor said. "You've let me finger-fuck you twice, it's the least you can do for me."

It dawned on Maria that his "medical procedure" was all bunk. If she had had any doubt about her standing, it had evaporated now. She was a *puta* and a stupid one at that. Tears flowed down her cheeks but she didn't stop the doctor when he reached around behind her head and pulled her mouth to his cock. She opened up and took him inside and gave him the best blowjob she could through her tears.

She was getting better at being a whore, she realized, when the doctor gasped and she felt his seed spray into her mouth. She swallowed, grimacing at the taste and hoping Mr. Reynolds didn't notice.

Of course he did.

"Do you want to spank her for that reaction or shall I?"

"I'll do it," Dr. Smith said at once. "But I'm going to save it until tomorrow."

Jason nodded. "Very well."

The doctor gathered up his things and left. Maria continued to sprawl on the bed and cry. Jason gathered up her clothes and tossed them on the bed. "Tomorrow," he said, slipping his belt loose from his pants, "I don't want you to be wearing panties all day. If I catch you with panties, I'll whip you." For emphasis, he slapped the folded belt against his palm. She jumped with the sound it made.

Maria pulled on her clothes, her tear-streaked face averted from Jason's. When she was finished, he pulled four hundred from his wallet and handed it over. "For two blowjobs," he said.

She could only nod and shuffle out.

CHAPTER SIX

Jason went downstairs the next morning at ten and found Maria on the seventh floor. As soon as he closed the door of the room she was cleaning, he waved his hands at her and she lifted her dress to show him she was naked underneath.

He smiled. "Good girl."

He came forward and reached between her legs. "Have you come since yesterday?"

She closed her eyes and shook her head. "Nooo," she breathed as his fingers rubbed against her. She was quickly wet. He kept it up, watching her face until she seemed on the verge of an orgasm, then he pulled away.

She moaned.

"Good, I want you on edge for this afternoon. Don't you dare come, you understand?"

She nodded. He left her there, still holding her dress up.

An hour and a half later, he returned and found her in another room. He repeated his actions, making her display herself and bringing her to the brink of an orgasm.

When he found her around two o'clock, he made her remove her clothes entirely. She balked, and he slid his belt from his pants. Maria quickly obeyed. When she was naked, he rubbed her pussy until she was gasping. This time, he took her bra with him as he left. She looked stricken.

At five, Dr. Smith was helping himself to his second bourbon and Jason was sipping bottled water from the wet bar. Both men were excited for this was the day they would get to fuck Jason's little whore.

"I can't wait to get into her. She nearly pulled my fingers off! There's nothing like a nineteen-year-old pussy."

"Yep. She's great." For some reason, now that he'd won his cruel little game, he was having second thoughts. Maybe it had been too easy. Or maybe Maria was just too naïve, too trusting. It hadn't been much of a contest. He knew if he had tried it with a more sophisticated woman, he'd be in jail right now or facing a lawsuit.

Maybe it was that Maria was such a perfect victim, offering herself up time and again when any other woman would've fled. Jason began to wonder if she secretly liked it, the way he treated her. She protested every step of the way, but she never bailed out on him.

That was odd, wasn't it?

The knock came at the door and Jason pushed it from his mind. He winked at Dr. Smith and went to the door, the doctor right behind. He opened it and Maria stood there in her ugly uniform.

"Well?"

Maria's face turned bright red even as she reached down and pulled up her dress, showing both of them her bare pussy. Jason could see was already wet from all the attention she'd been getting that day. Suddenly, a door opened down the hall and a man came out, whistling. She started to lower her dress, but Jason just shook his head. Her expression was priceless.

The man gaped and he stopped to stare. "Jeez—where can I get service like that?"

"What room are you in?" Jason asked.

"Twelve-thirty-two. You gonna send her over?"

Maria silently begged him. "I don't know. I'll see if she's free." To Maria, he said, "You may lower your dress."

She obeyed at once, gratitude washing over her face.

The man shook his head and gave a low whistle. "That's something. Let me know, huh? I'll be back around seven." He went on down the hall.

Jason stepped aside and let Maria in. She nearly collapsed on the floor inside the door. Dr. Smith grabbed her around the waist, holding her up.

"Whoa there, sweetie! Here, sit down." He led her to the bed and she sat.

"Why don't you help her get out of her clothes?"

Dr. Smith nodded. He unzipped her dress and pulled it over her head and whistled when he saw she was wearing nothing but those thigh-high stockings. "Pretty!"

"You want her to take those off or leave them on?"

"Oh, I like them on. Makes her look sexier."

"Very well. Maria, the doctor needs to give you your pill and examine you, okay?"

Her mouth came open and she nodded. She knew what was in store and she felt resigned to it. Dr. Smith gave her the pill and she swallowed it down. Maria noted he didn't bother to test her heart or lungs, nor did he put on rubber gloves. He pushed her back onto the pillows and spread her legs. She watched as he slid two fingers into her pussy and began to stroke her. When she started to react, he leaned forward and licked at her swollen clit.

"Ohhhhh!" she moaned, her pussy spasming around his fingers.

"Hey, did you just come?"

"*Lo siento*, Dr. Smith. Mr. Reynolds kept me…He made me…" she shook her head as her English failed her.

"Well, I guess it's time for your punishment."

She paled. "*Que?*"

"Remember yesterday when you made a face?" Jason put in. "The doctor gets to spank you now." He turned toward him. "What do you prefer, your hand or a belt?"

"My hand might get too sore. I'd better use a belt." He slipped his belt free from the loops and Maria gasped.

"Not too hard, right doc? We don't want her ass too sore."

"Right." He pulled Maria over onto her stomach. She writhed and cried even before he struck her. The first blow cracked loudly against her cheeks and both men admired the red mark. Dr. Smith hit her three more times before he stopped. Both men's cocks were rock hard by now.

Dr. Smith quickly unzipped his pants and slid them down his legs. His boxer shorts followed. His hard cock jutted out. He turned Maria onto her back and she looked at him with alarm. She turned to Jason, panic in her voice. "But Mr. Reynolds! I thought you..."

"Oh, that's right, Doc. You need to pay her three hundred."

Even as he said it, Jason felt the cruelty of the remark. He tried to dismiss it from his mind. After all, he was superior to this little tart and he had proved it, in spades.

Dr. Smith fished his wallet out of his pants as Jason watched Maria's reaction. He was now pimping her out and there was no doubt left about what she had become. Tears flowed from her eyes as the doctor laid three one-hundred dollar bills on the pillow next to her and crawled between her legs. She lay limply, not fighting him or protesting. Jason could see she had accepted her corruption: She was his whore and she would do what he wanted.

So why did he feel so bad about it?

Maria felt the doctor's cock slide into her and tried not to react. That didn't last long.

"Hey, come on," the doc said. "Don't just lie there. Pretend you like it."

"Unless you want to be punished again," Jason said, watching her from the other bed.

Maria looked over, startled. She allowed her pussy to respond, squeezing his cock and feeling sudden waves of pleasure ripple through her.

"Oh yeah, there she goes! Ohhh!" The doctor began to rut with her and she felt his cock reach all the way to her cervix. Her own body betrayed her as she came once, then twice before she felt the man empty his seed within her. She cried for her lost virginity and for what Mr. Reynolds had made her.

His *puta.*

But she cried most of all for what she had done to herself.

When the doctor rolled off of her, Jason took his place. He fucked her too, depositing his seed inside her soiled pussy. They rested for a few minutes and then both men made her suck them to hardness so they could fuck her again. She found herself going through the motions with Mr. Reynolds until he pulled away from her in disgust.

"You call that a blowjob? I taught you better than that!"

"Please, sir, I'm so tired!"

"That's no excuse." He made Dr. Smith hold her down and he whipped her ass with his belt four more times. The pain woke her from her ennui and Maria performed much better from that point on. They wanted her not just to lay there or be passive—they wanted her to make them feel good, to put energy into her work.

That's what it was. Her work. It paid very well, of course. Far better than she could make as a maid. She already had enough to bring Lola over the border and she had made initial inquiries.

Not surprisingly, a part of her liked imagining she was Mr. Reynolds' girlfriend. But not when he made her fuck this other man. She could not explain to herself why she kept showing up or why she allowed this man to humiliate her so. It had to be more than just the money he paid her. Maybe she really was a *puta*, after all, despite how she'd been raised. She worried that Lola might find out.

She was draped over the edge of the bed and Dr. Smith slipped his cock into her again. She came, despite herself and came again when Mr. Reynolds took his place. They were both tired finally and they sent her into the bathroom to shower.

It felt good to be alone for a few minutes and she luxuriated in the hot water. The shower at her aunt's apartment trickled in comparison. When she stepped out, she found both men sitting on the bed, drinking. They had gotten dressed. She was still naked, of course.

She padded in and Dr. Smith asked her if she wanted a drink. She shook her head. She had never liked the taste.

Mr. Reynolds looked at his watch. "Hey, it's after seven. Why don't you run down to apartment twelve-thirty-two and ask that nice man if he wants a fuck or a blowjob."

Maria stared at him, her face turning white.

"Tell him it's two hundred for a blowjob and five hundred for a fuck. If that's too much for him, then come on back. Don't let him talk you into any discounts."

Maria fought the panic rising within her. "Please, sir. I want to stay. You fuck me again, okay?"

Mr. Reynolds shook his head. "Go."

She bent down to pick up her dress and Mr. Reynolds put his foot on it. "Just go like that. You need to advertise."

"No! No can be *en cueros!*" She put her face in her hands.

"Relax, this floor is nearly deserted. You'll be fine. Go." He picked up the belt.

Maria rose to her feet, feeling her legs shaking under her. She went to the door and peeked out. The corridor was empty. She looked back and noticed an odd expression on Mr. Reynolds' face.

"Wait." Mr. Reynolds turned to the doctor. "Uh, doc, can you excuse us?"

"What? Oh, sure." Dr. Smith nodded to her and left, his hands stroking her shoulder as he passed by.

She turned to look at Mr. Reynolds. "Maria…" He seemed to be wrestling with himself. "Forget it. About that other man. I just wanted to see if you'd do it."

"You make me. I no want to."

"You can get dressed now."

As Maria put on her clothes, she added up how much her whoring had earned. She had more than three thousand as of last night when she had counted it in her room at her aunt's apartment. Today, she made…she stopped.

"Hey!"

"What?"

"You owe me money too! For fuckings and blowjobs!"

Mr. Reynolds shook his head and she noticed that hard expression had returned. "Yeah, but as your pimp, I get that for free now."

Her mouth dropped open. "You shit!" She quickly tossed her dress over her head, not bothering with her stockings. She stormed out of the room.

The door slammed.

Jason stood there, feeling another pang of conscience. What was this? What happened to the game? The superiority he felt? Truth was, he did feel like a shit. He had proved he could turn Maria into a whore, but to what end? He was leaving day after tomorrow and his plan had been to pay her off with another five hundred or so and never think about her again. But when he was about to send her down the hall to that stranger's room, it had hit him just how despicable a man he had become. There was no excuse for it—he was just as bad as all those "regular people" had thought he was. His game simply proved it.

And now he had taken an innocent girl, a girl who really represented what was good about humanity, and turned her into something cheap. He suddenly realized he didn't want to leave her. She was a better person than he was and he wanted her in her life. Maybe some of that goodness might rub off on him. Or was that just guilt talking?

"Jesus," he said aloud. "I must really be an asshole."

He paced for an hour, trying to sort out his feelings. He could imagine Maria at her apartment right now, crying and blaming herself for becoming "Mr. Reynolds' whore." But it was her innocence that led her down that path more than her greed. She never wanted the money for herself—she wanted it to bring her sister to America.

The more he thought about it, the worse he felt.

CHAPTER SEVEN

The next morning, after a near-sleepless night, he went down to the seventh floor to find Maria and apologize. He spotted the cart and came into the room, only to stop short, surprised. A heavyset Latina woman about fifty was vacuuming. When she saw him staring, she shut off the machine.

"Yes, sir?"

"Uh, I'm looking for Maria..."

"Oh! She quit. Very suddenly too. Made me angry."

Oh shit, he thought. It's all my fault.

He saw her nametag: Esmeralda. "Are you the head maid?"

"Yes. Is there something you need, sir?"

"Yes. I need to find Maria." Her eyes grew hard and he quickly thought of an excuse. "You see, I was helping her bring Lola to the U.S., but there's been a hang up and I need to talk to her about it."

At the mention of Maria's sister, the woman's face softened. "Yes, she has been saving for that. You're helping her?"

"Yes, we're hoping to bring Lola up much sooner. I, uh, have some jobs for them. That's why she quit, because she and Lola have other jobs lined up. But there's a small problem and I need to talk to her first."

"Why she no tell me!? She leave so sudden!"

"Well, I told her not to say until it was more of a sure thing. Please, can you give me her address or phone number?"

The maid sighed and walked past him to her cart. He followed. She found a small notebook and read off her aunt's phone number.

"Thank you. Uh, do you have her address as well?" He held up a fifty, which she pocketed quickly. She read off her address and Jason wrote it down.

He walked down the corridor, cell phone in hand, trying to think of what to say. He waited until he was back in his room before he dialed.

No one answered.

Damnit!

Now he was worried. Had Maria run away? Hurt herself? She was in a shaky emotional state and it was his fault. His game had been so stupid and foolish! He was playing with a girl's life here!

All because you got fucking BORED? Because you were afraid you'd drink again?

Jason pocketed Maria's pills, went downstairs and hailed a cab.

Maria's aunt lived in Redlands, about twenty miles to the south. Jason ordered the cab to hurry and he worried he might already be too late. If she hurt herself, he'd never forgive himself.

He threw some money at the cabby and raced into the dilapidated apartment complex. He found Apartment 906 on the second floor and knocked.

No answer. He tried again, hoping she was home and not answering her phone. He wasn't about to give up. More than once, a neighbor peered at him from the crack of their doors, but Jason tried to ignore them. He knew someone might be calling the manager soon to complain about the wild man banging on the door.

Suddenly, the door in front of him opened a crack and Maria's face peered out. She looked ashen and worn down. When she saw it was him, she slammed it again.

"Please, Maria! I've made a big mistake! I'm so sorry! I need to talk to you, please! Open the door!"

For a long moment, Jason was afraid she'd keep him out, but finally the door opened again and she stepped back to allow him inside. The place was small, dingy and cramped. But he didn't care about that, he only had eyes for Maria. She looked quite different from yesterday, eyes more sunken and face pale. Something had broken inside of her. Even now, she was starting to get undressed, stripping off her cheap T-shirt and unbuckling her jeans.

He was shocked. "Wait."

She paused. "You no want to fuck your *puta?*"

Remorse washed over him. "No. I'm so sorry. I was an ass." He rubbed his head, trying to figure a way he could explain. But how could he explain away the loss of her virginity, the most precious gift a young girl has to offer?

"Please, Maria. Put on your shirt and sit down." He went and sat on the lumpy couch. She eyed him for a long time before she slipped her shirt back on and sat down next to him.

"That stupid game," he began. "You've got to understand. I am an alcoholic. I drank all the time. I went into rehab—you understand rehab?"

She nodded, her face expressionless.

"When I came out, I couldn't do anything I used to do. I had no friends, no fun. I was afraid to start drinking again. So I did a cruel and stupid thing—I decided to play a stupid game that wound up hurting you badly."

She stared at him. "You never love me—all just game?"

Jason wasn't going to lie to her now. "Yeah—I mean, up until yesterday. When I made you fuck Dr. Smith, I felt jealous. I was angry at myself. I tried to pretend otherwise. I had convinced myself it was still part of the game, but I realized what a horrible man I'd become. It was a cruel game. I guess I'm kind of an asshole. You know asshole?"

The edge of her mouth twitched. *"Boludo. Tu es boludo."*

"Yeah, that sounds about right." He took a breath. "The thing is, when I realized what a shit I've been, I went looking for you and found you had quit."

She shrugged. "I find new job."

"That's what I wanted to talk to you about. I know you have enough money now to bring Lola over. But what then? Your money won't last—and from the looks of this place, you can't all fit." He took a deep breath. "I have a solution for you, if you want. A new job."

"New job?" Her eyes narrowed. "As your *puta*?"

"No! I need a maid and a part-time cook at my apartment in New York. You'd be well paid and I'm often gone a lot, so you'd have the run of the place."

She scoffed. "Live-in *puta*."

"I don't deny that I really like making love to you, but *puta*? No. The game is over. You'd be like my girlfriend in a lot of ways."

Maria thought about that. "Girlfriend? Why you do that?"

"Because I took something valuable from you. And I want to make it right."

She bit her lip and Jason saw the tears filling up her eyes and felt like a shit all over again.

"What about Lola?"

"She can live there too. You'd have to share a room, but that would be all right, wouldn't it?"

"You make her your *puta* too?"

"No. I won't. She could help you around the place." He tried not to think about having two beautiful girls around his place. He wasn't sure he was man enough to resist the temptation. *I'll deal with that later*, he thought.

"I don't know. I don't like you right now."

"I know. But what else will you do? Go to work at another hotel for six bucks an hour?"

"How much you pay?"

"Twice that for each of you, plus you'll have free room and board. And I'll help Lola get into a school, if she wants."

She stared at him. "I think, okay?"

"Okay. But I'm leaving tomorrow at noon. You come by my hotel room and let me know, okay?"

She didn't say no, but she didn't say yes, either. "I think, okay?" she repeated and that would have to do. Jason rose and gave one more apology and left her there on the couch. On his way to the door, he paused, remembering her pills. Should he even leave them? Would she understand that he wanted to make love to her again? He took them out of his pocket and lay them on the arm of a chair.

He turned back to her and said, "I should never have made you have sex with Dr. Smith. Of all the things I did, that's what I regret the most."

Maria didn't move. She watched him as he slipped out the door.

By eleven-thirty the next morning, Jason feared she wouldn't show. At last the knock came to his door and he opened it to see Maria standing there, dressed in her jeans and T-shirt. She looked wonderful to him.

He invited her in and she eased past him.

"You want me to take off clothes?" she asked.

"No!" Then he saw her wry smile and he laughed. "Okay, you got me."

He came forward and hugged her. She didn't resist.

"Have you decided to come to New York?"

"*Sí*. But you take care of me? And Lola? You no throw us out later?"

"No, I won't throw you out later. If you decide you want to leave, I'll pay to move you both back here to live with your aunt, okay?"

"Okay," Maria said. She pulled away and looked at him. "You still shit for what you did."

"I know. I don't blame you for being angry. I'm surprised you are even here."

She looked away. "I too. I not rich. But I always hope to get good job, for Lola. You bad man, but I see good in you, no? I think you treat me better now."

"Yes, I promise." But he had to ask. "Uh, Maria..."

Her dark eyes locked onto his. *"Sí?"*

"Look, I'll admit it—I love being around you. Just seeing you makes me smile. And I hated sharing with Dr. Smith. That will never happen again. But if you come live with me, I know I'll want to make love to you again. I'm just being honest here."

Maria stared at him. *"No puta?"*

"No puta."

She snuggled into his arms. "Maybe."

Jason felt relief wash over him. He didn't know how it would work out between them, for they really were quite different. But he liked her and that would be enough for now.

"On one condition, though."

She looked up, expectantly.

"Don't let me drink. I'm a real asshole when I drink."

She laughed.

STRIPPED AND ABUSED

Diane Landis was shoved into the dimly lit cell. She stumbled against the edge of the bed.

"Hey! Don't be so rough!" She fought her panic with bravado, but her quivering voice betrayed her.

"You'll stay here until you can post bail," the guard said. He started to slam the steel door.

"Wait! What about my phone call!" How did they expect her to post bail if they wouldn't let her call her parents? Her dad was a lawyer; he'd know what to do.

The guard just smiled and slammed the door in her face.

"You fucker!" She screamed. She pounded on the door, shouting out her frustrations until she finally collapsed weeping on the bed. When she recovered sufficiently to try to overcome her fear, her anger set in.

She'd been picked up on some rinky-dink traffic violation in this god-forsaken hick town somewhere in backwards Mississippi and tossed in jail without so much as a whiff of *habeous corpus.*

They can't do that! This is fucking America!

Diane was sure she'd see a judge tomorrow and then heads would roll! When her dad found out, he'd own this fucking town.

She sat up and looked around her. Her brow furrowed. This looked like no cell she'd ever seen on TV shows. For one, it had a twin bed, not a cot with a thin mattress. It was shoved up into the far corner of the small cell. There was a white fitted sheet on it but no blanket. It did have two very large pillows, which made it look almost cheery. But it seemed large for the room. In fact, the room was only about eighteen inches longer than the bed and eighteen inches wider, giving her a narrow walkway by the door and along one side. She glanced up at the far end and spotted a small chemical toilet. In a jail cell, she would have expected real plumbing, not some cheap camping john.

And then there was the corridor leading to her cell, she remembered. She expected to see bars, not cold cement walls and steel doors with slots in them. Diane looked up; her slot was closed at the moment.

Perhaps this cell block had been converted from some other use, she mused. A way for the county to save money. Yeah, that must be it. Cheap bastards.

Her eye caught something high up on the wall and she froze, pulling her jean jacket closer around her torso. It was a small black camera lens, mounted high up behind Plexiglas. She looked around and spotted one more. Both appeared to be aimed at the bed.

Diane suddenly felt very creepy.

She raised her hand and flipped off the cameras, one at a time, then flounced on the bed. She would have to sleep in her clothes to avoid giving them a peep show. But what about when she had to use the toilet? She shivered and hugged herself tightly.

She sat up again and looked at the wall near the door. There was something odd about it. She approached it. Next to the door was a push button, like a light switch you'd find in an old-fashioned hotel. Inset in the wall above it were two round dark glass disks, each about the size of a quarter. She pushed the button. Nothing happened. No one came.

Huh. She sat back on the bed and put her head in her hands. Diane guessed it must be around nine o'clock. The cops had pulled her over just after dark, which fell around eight this time of year. She couldn't believe it when one of them—a brute of a yokel with the last name Darkins on his uniform shirt—slapped the handcuffs on her.

"Hey!" she had said. "Why don't you just write me a ticket and let me go!" Not that she'd pay it! She had expected to be long gone out of this state by morning.

But they ignored her. Darkins had tossed her in the back of his cruiser like some criminal and she watched as he got into her car, made a u-turn and followed the patrol unit as the second cop drove back to the station.

"Hey! What the hell's going on?" Diane asked him. He was a typical overweight "good ol' boy" with short dark hair. She didn't see his nametag, but thought he was probably Darkins' second cousin—don't they all inbreed in these backwoods towns? He said nothing.

Well, she thought as she fought her panic, at least my car will be nearby and not left by the side of the road where it could be stolen or stripped. It had all her luggage in the trunk, whatever she could pack quickly before her bastard of a husband had returned home.

She had been on her way back to live with her parents—just temporarily!—until she could get back on her feet. Damn! Her mother had told her not to marry David.

"I just got a feeling," she'd say when Diane asked her why.

But she had married him anyway and within two years it all went to hell. He went from being a nice guy who worshipped the ground she walked on to a controlling, abusive jerk. She might've stuck it out if he had agreed to counseling but he had refused. When he started accusing her of cheating on him with the mailman, the paper boy and her boss at the office, she knew it was time to go.

She had waited until he had left for work, packed up as much as she could fit into her car and hit the road. She didn't even leave him a note. He didn't deserve one.

Diane had meant to call her parents, to warn them she was coming, but she'd been so embarrassed, she had just decided to show up. Even though her mom would want to say, "I told you so," Diane knew she'd just give her a big hug and welcome her home.

Except now, she realized, no one knew where the hell she was. *I'm not even sure I do,* she thought.

With nothing else to do, she curled up and tried to get some sleep.

The next morning—she assumed it was morning, for the cell had no windows—Diane woke up groggily and looked around. Nothing had changed, except the light overhead was brighter. She could see everything in her cell more clearly now.

But she had a more pressing need. Her bladder was full and she held it as long as she could before finally approaching the small toilet. Turning around, she saw the unblinking eye of the camera, just waiting for her. She slipped off her jacket and placed the collar in her mouth so it would hang down and cover her privates. Diane unbuckled her jeans and yanked down her panties, pleased to notice the camera couldn't see anything. As she sat and peed, she remembered the other one, located right above. She craned her head around and saw it was pointing down. Must've gotten a pretty good view of her ass. She flipped it off.

When she rose, she noticed there was no toilet paper. "Dammit!" she cried to the room. "What kind of shithole are you running here?"

She had to ease her panties up against herself without wiping, making her grimace.

Diane waited on the edge of the bed for the guard to return and take her to court. Her stomach growled. Time passed slowly. They had taken her watch, keys and cell phone. They even took her shoelaces—like she would kill herself over a traffic ticket!

She wished she had a newspaper to read. A crossword—anything! This sitting and waiting was aggravating.

She got up again and approached the strange switch. She pressed it again and again, hoping a light was going on at a guard's station. It didn't seem to be doing anything and she gave up after a while.

Diane sat there for hours, alternately pacing, sitting and pounding on the door. She heard nothing. Did they forget about her in here? Dammit, she was thirsty too. Her throat was dry and her lips felt cracked. There wasn't so much as a spigot to get a drink!

The day stretched on. This wasn't right. Something must be terribly wrong. Did the officers forget to tell them they had arrested someone? No, wait, they had turned her over to the ugly guard. He would know she was here.

It was odd that very little was said to her. Her fingerprints had been taken, and a mug shot. They had even showed it to her. She saw a young, frightened blonde woman she hardly recognized. Her eyes had seemed a bit wild.

"Hey!" she shouted again, kicking at the door with her unlaced tennis shoes. "Hey! You can't just leave me in here!"

She endured a long, depressing, thirsty day. She peed just once more before the lights began to go dim, telling her it was night once again. They had left her in here all day with no food or water! Her stomach ached with hunger and she had trouble keeping her fear at bay.

Finally, she fell asleep on her bed, exhausted and desperate.

When the lights rose again in the "morning," Diane was beside herself. Her throat was parched and she knew the human body could live for weeks without food, but only three days without water. She had endured a little over a day. They had better come today or tomorrow or she might die.

How could they allow that?

She peed just a trickle, for her body had little to give. This time, she didn't try to hide herself—she was too far gone for modesty. And what about when she had to poop? There was still no toilet paper! She grimaced at the thought.

What she wouldn't give for a nice big bottle of water! One of those quart-sized ones, frosty and cold from the fridge. She could almost taste it going down her throat, easing her thirst and making her feel human again.

Diane figured she probably stank by now. Wouldn't they even take her out for a shower? If they did, she could drink the water and everything would be all right. Her stomach growled again and she started thinking of food. A juicy Big Mac with fries—and a frosty shake, of course!

She lay on the bed, staring at the ceiling, waiting to be called to court. Her body seemed to have grown considerably weaker in just one day, but she suspected that was probably psychological. Why, on TV shows, she had seen stories about men who had survived days in the desert with nothing to eat and little to drink!

Diane fell asleep and dreamt fitfully. In one dream, she was arguing with David, who had accused her of fucking his best friend Charlie. She had denied it, of course and was begging him for the bottle of water he held out of reach.

"Please, David, just let me have a sip. I'll tell you everything you want to know."

"Will you tell me about fucking Charlie? Will you?" David demanded.

"I didn't! But if that's what it takes to get water, then okay, you crazy bastard! I was fucking him! We fucked in the car, we fucked on the couch. We even fucked on the front lawn! Now can I have some water?"

David started to say something sarcastic and hurtful when there came a bang from the front of the house. David turned toward it and Diane followed his gaze. They heard a voice and she realized it wasn't in the dream—it was in her cell! She came awake at once, struggling to her feet, her lips dry. The slot in the door was open and the ugly guard's face appeared.

"Please! Water! I need water! I'm dying!"

The guard, a tall man with a scar along one cheek, laughed. "Oh, you won't die. We wouldn't allow that."

"Please! I have a right to a phone call! And water and food! You can't keep me her indefinitely! I haven't even been arraigned yet!" It hurt her mouth to talk, yet the words tumbled out of her.

Scarface held up a bottle of water. Diane's eyes grew large. "Is this what you want?"

"Yes! Yes, please!" She lunged for the slot and the guard pulled back, keeping the bottle up so she could see it. "Why are you being so mean?" she asked.

The guard nodded. "Sorry about that. I just wanted to make sure I had your full attention, so I can explain some things to you."

Diane hung on to the slot, keeping her eyes just above the edge. "What? What do you mean?"

"You've been found guilty..." he started.

"What! I haven't even seen a judge! Or a lawyer! I demand a trial!"

"Oh, you had a trial—you just weren't there. Are you going to listen or should I come back, say, tomorrow?"

"No, no," she said quietly, her eyes never leaving the bottle of water. "I'll be quiet."

"Okay. You were found guilty of speeding, reckless endangerment, resisting arrest..."

"What! I never resisted arrest!" I wasn't driving recklessly, either, she thought.

"I guess I'll have to come back later, when you're more cooperative." Scarface shrugged his shoulders and waved her away from the door. He started to close it on her fingers and she had to pull them back. It slammed shut.

"Wait! Don't go! I need water!" She heard his boots echoing down the corridor and she flopped on the bed and sobbed.

She endured another long day with nothing to do but think about her own mortality. Her tongue was thick in her mouth and she had trouble organizing her thoughts. When the lights dimmed, telling her she'd have to wait another night for relief, she cried.

Why were they being so mean?

Diane lay limply on the bed as the lights came back up again. Another morning. She could barely move. Her mouth was so dry, she really believed she might die today. This was her third day without water. She didn't have much time left.

She didn't need to use the potty. Pulling herself upright, she sat and stared at the wall opposite the bed. This time, Scarface didn't keep her waiting long. She heard his footsteps and the grating of the slot opening and she glanced up, too weak to rise.

"Are you more cooperative today?"

Diane just nodded dully.

"Good. Now let me explain the sentence you've been given."

She actually felt her mouth open to protest and immediately shut it again. The guard noticed and he chuckled.

"Good girl. You're learning. Now here's the deal. The Beaumont County circuit judge has sentenced you to ninety days in jail—"

"Ninety days?" she croaked. That seemed excessive for a traffic ticket. Surely she would be missed during that time!

"Yes, ninety days. But this isn't one of those four-star jails you probably have back home, no siree. Here, you have to work, you unnerstand?"

"Work?" She visualized herself in the hot sun, breaking rocks.

"Yes. If you want food and water..." he held up that magic bottle of water again and Diane's mouth dropped open. "...you'll have to earn it, okay?"

She nodded, waiting.

"Good girl. Now if you look to your left, you'll see a switch on the wall."

Diane looked over, remembering the switch she had pressed uselessly so many times. Now there were two lights above the switch—one red, one green. She licked her chapped lips and nodded again. Then the green light went out.

"Here's the deal. When you see a red light come on, that means you have the opportunity to earn something. It could be this bottle of water. It could be food. It could be a shower or other privileges. If you agree to work, you come over and push the button. Easy, huh?"

Diane nodded again. She struggled to her feet and pushed the switch under the darkened circle of glass. The red light went out and the green light lit up.

"Good! You're learning quick."

She reached up her hand toward the slot, expecting him to hand through the small bottle of water.

"Ohhh, wait—you haven't earned it yet. You've just indicated your willingness to earn it."

Diane stood there, stupidly and stared at him.

"Okay, for this bottle of water..." he shook it and it sounded musical to her. "...you just have to take off all your clothes and do a little sexy dance for the cameras."

Diane shrank back. "Noooooo!" she moaned.

"Suit yourself," he said and slid the slot closed.

"Nooooooooo!" Her voice was pitched higher now, like the keening of a woman who had just suffered a great loss. She heard his boots clomp down the corridor.

Without even thinking about it, she yanked off her jacket and began to unbutton her blouse. She imagined a little stripper's tune in her head as she bumped and grinded her way to removing the blouse in a sexy way. She tossed it on the bed and reached around behind to unfasten her bra. Turning this way and that, she showed both cameras her bare back before dropping her bra and flashing her breasts.

She was running on adrenalin and she knew her body would collapse soon.

Next came the jeans. Wiggling her hips, Diane unzipped them and pulled them down to her thighs, leaving her panties in place. She sat on the bed and pulled the legs free and tossed the pants onto a corner of the bed. Standing again, she wiggled her hips again for both cameras and eased her panties off her hips, exposing her narrow strip of hair leading to the incurving line of her vagina. She stepped out of them and flung them into the air, showing her nakedness off like a burlesque dancer.

Exhausted, Diane sank down onto the bed and began to cry. She had no tears, so it was a very dry cry.

Within five minutes, she heard Scarface return. She got up and waited by the door. The slot came open and the bottle was thrust through. "You did great, Diane! You really gave us a good show! Enjoy!"

She grabbed it and twisted off the cap and drank it in one long swallow, feeling her strength return. When it was gone and she turned, she saw Scarface peering at her naked body through the slot and turned her back.

"Oh, too late for that. You should see the resolution on those cameras! Why, we could read the word on that cute little tattoo you have right above your ass!"

She reached around in embarrassment and felt the long-forgotten mark. It said "David" in script. He had one that said, "Diane" on his upper arm. That had been a long time ago when they had been crazy in love.

Suddenly, she realized she was still giving the cameras a show. She grabbed her clothes and put them back on, while Scarface laughed from the door. "Oh, honey, you're so modest all of a sudden!"

Now that her thirst was temporarily quenched, she had another pressing need. "Please, can I get something to eat? Oh, and maybe, um, some toilet paper?"

"Everything must be earned. Now you got your water, what will you do for a nice meal?" Before she could speak, he went on, "But, oh, look! The red light's out. That means it's not time yet for another reward."

The slot slammed and he went away. Diane sat on the bed and cried.

She was thirsty again an hour later when the red light went on. She ran to the switch and started to press it and hesitated. It occurred to her she didn't know what she was agreeing to do. Whatever it was, it would be degrading and humiliating. It might even involve rape, she thought. If she pressed it and refused to do whatever it was, would they punish her? Well, of course they'd withhold whatever it is she was "working" for, but would they get angry and add to her punishments? She couldn't go for another three days without water!

Diane realized they had her by the short hairs and she would have to do whatever it took to survive. Once she got out, then she could sic her father the lawyer on them. She pressed the button. Sitting on the bed, she waited, her heart pounding, to hear what she'd have to do this time.

Scarface returned. The slot went back. "Good girl!" he said in that maddingly cheerful voice. "That light was to earn food." He held up a hot dog wrapped in a napkin. "Since you've agreed to work, this time we want you to strip, lean those pillows up against the wall and masturbate. Be very vocal and act like you're enjoying it."

Diane stared at him. "No!" The word came out automatically. "You can't make me do that!"

"But you agreed!" Scarface said. "Don't push the button unless you're going to agree."

"I didn't know what I was agreeing to!" She shouted.

"That's part of the fun," he said. "Now you get to see what happens when you break the rules."

The door clanked and began to open and Diane prepared herself to throw her body at the guard. Maybe she could slip past him and run down the corridor to...she remembered the steel door at the end when she had first come in and realized she'd have to grab his keys on the way by. Her odds of success diminished considerably.

When the door opened she shot forward only to run into not only the solid body of Scarface, but also another guard! They grabbed her easily and hauled her kicking and screaming back to the bed. Scarface held her arms while the other guard proceeded to rip her pants down to her thighs, panties too. Then he held her legs and Scarface unbuckled his belt and slipped it from the loops.

Diane knew what was about to happen and tried to wiggle free. They were far too strong.

Whack! The belt slapped hard against her bare upturned ass. Whack! She writhed in pain, screaming and begging. Whack! Whack! Whack! The pain overwhelmed her and she passed out for a moment. When she came too, both guards had simply waited for her to awaken and started anew.

Whack! Whack! The blows went on and on. How many times were they going to spank her like this? This was humiliating and painful. When they finally stopped, Diane could hardly move. They let her go and her hands went back to touch her fiery ass and gasped with pain.

"That's twenty strokes for pushing the button and not following through. Don't be a tease, girl, or you'll pay the consequences."

He got up and bent down near the door and picked up the hot dog, which seemed a little worse for the wear. The edge of one boot carved a semi-circle out of the middle. "Ohh, looks like your hot dog got stepped on. Too bad."

He held it out to her. "You pressed the button. I'm sure you'd like to eat. So get busy." He paused. "Unless you'd like twenty more with the belt."

She shook her head. Without pulling up her pants, she scooted up against the wall, grimacing with pain when her ass touched the sheets. "Ow, it really hurts," she said, lifting it up. Her pussy was on display for the two guards and there was nothing she could do about it.

"You're wasting time," the second guard said. He was more muscular and broad in the shoulders. Unlike Scarface, his head was shaved bald. She nicknamed him Curly.

Diane pulled her jeans off and tried to ignore the pain shooting up from her bottom. When she finally was able to sit still, her back up against the pillows, she took in a shuddering breath and reached between her legs. Her fingers started to stroke her dry slit, trying to draw moisture from it. The last thing she wanted to do was put on a show for these men.

She rubbed, not feeling much of anything. Maybe they'll accept just the actions, not a full-on climax. But as she mechanically rubbed, she could tell the guards were growing impatient.

"Come on!" Scarface finally said. "You can do better than that! I want to see a real earth-shattering come!"

"I'm trying," she begged. "It's hard with you watching me like this."

"Too bad. You could've done it for the cameras—and without the whipping," Curly said.

Diane tried harder, closing her eyes to blot out the leering guards. Finally, she felt some moisture begin to leak from her slit and she drew it up to her clit. A small thrill went through her. She believed she might be able to come now. Just needed a few more minutes...

"You're pathetic," Scarface said, getting up. He still had the hot dog.

"Please! I was almost there!"

"Too bad. You're boring us." Both guards got up and went out the door, slamming it behind her. Diane, still half naked, cried when she realized she wasn't going to be allowed to eat for the third day in a row.

And now she was thirsty again. She tried to put on her pants but her ass hurt too much. So she just draped her jean jacket over her as she lay on the bed on her stomach.

The red light remained off all night. She knew, because she woke up often to check on it. Her stomach seemed to have given up on her and no longer growled, but her throat wasn't about to. She was thirsty almost to the point of hallucinations.

When the lights went up in her cell, Diane rose and got dressed, wrinkling her nose in disgust at the dirty panties she had to wear. She finally tossed them into a corner. Her jeans seemed to scrape against her tender ass, but he she managed to get them on. Diane sat on the edge of the bed, watching for the light. When the red light clicked on, she dove for the switch and hit it, illuminating the green light. Then she sat back and waited.

Scarface appeared at the slot. "Smart girl. Now here's the deal. I have another bottle of water..." He held it up.

Yes! she thought.

"...and a fried egg sandwich." He showed her that too. "You agreed to work for them, so I hope we're not going to have to punish you for refusing like last time."

She shook her head.

"Good. For the water, I want to make a trade. Your blouse and bra. Shove them through the slot."

Diane only thought about it for a minute before standing up and stripping off her stained blouse and bra and shoving them through to fall at Scarface's feet. "Good." He handed her the bottle. She unscrewed the top and drank half of it, vowing to save the rest for later.

"Now, for the egg sandwich, I want your pants and panties."

She had expected that. She still had her jean jacket, which would provide some modesty. And her shoes. Besides, she told herself, those panties were really dirty now anyway. Diane found her panties and shoved them through the slot. Then she kicked off her shoes, stripped her jeans off and shoved them through as well.

"Smart girl." He passed the sandwich through. She devoured it in five bites. Then she drank the rest of the water to wash it down. So much for saving it, she thought.

Scarface leered at her and she turned away from him.

"Hey!" He barked.

She turned back. "Let me see you, slut."

Her face burned. She wanted to cover herself with her jacket but guessed it would only make him mad. She didn't want to endure another spanking. He stared at her for a few minutes, then laughed and slid the slot closed.

Diane ran to the bed and covered herself with her jacket. Then she began to cry again.

She endured another long, lonely day. What made it worse, she knew what would happen next. Sure enough, the next morning, when she was hungry and thirsty all over again, the red light came on. She sat staring at it, knowing they'd ask for her jacket and shoes. Then she'd be completely naked—and at their mercy. For once her clothes were gone, what else would she have to trade for food and water? She shivered. She knew the answer to that.

Men. They were all alike. They loved the power, the abuse, the humiliation of women, whether they be strangers or friends. Even wives. Diane resolved to get it over with because she needed to keep her strength up. That was her only hope. Or maybe she was just fooling herself.

She went over and pressed the button. This time, Scarface offered her a bottle of water and a baloney sandwich.

"For the jacket and shoes," he sneered.

She stripped them off and tried to shove the jacket through the slot but it was too bulky. "Hang on, I'll open the door. Go sit on the bed, up against the wall."

She obeyed, watching the door open, her mouth watering. Scarface kicked her clothes into the hall and slammed the door before she could even move. She bounced off the bed and stood by the slot, half expecting him to keep the clothes and the food, but true to his word, he handed her both the sandwich and the bottle through the slot.

"You're doing fine. Only eighty-six days to go."

She blinked away tears. Then she crawled up onto the bed, one pillow behind her for support, the other in front providing some modesty as she ate her sandwich and drank most of her water. This time, she planned to save some.

The next day, she knew, would be horrible. But she told herself she wasn't a virgin. She'd sucked cock. She'd been fucked. She could handle it. Like a prostitute, she would trade part of her body in order to keep the rest alive. What was worse, she had to defecate that morning and without toilet paper, she felt incredibly soiled.

When the red light went on the next morning, Diane barely hesitated. She pressed the button and waited. Scarface was prompt, probably because he was looking forward to this day.

"My, don't you look sweet, naked as the day you were born."

"Please, I, uh, need, um, toilet paper."

"Aww, did the prisoner poop? You know, I thought I smelled sumtin' funny." He laughed out loud.

A flush darkened her skin. "It's not funny. Please. You can't possibly want me smelling like this. Please. I need a shower. And some food. And the toilet paper, of course."

"Aww! Three things you ask for now! And you don't seem to have anything left to trade."

"Come on, I'll give you a blowjob," she blustered. "Just as soon as I've had a shower. I really stink."

He nodded. "That's a lot to ask. For all that, you gotta give Chucky one too."

Chucky she assumed was the second guard. Curly. "Chucky? His name is Chucky?"

Sam grinned. "Yeah. He looks kinda like that doll in the movies, doesn't he?"

"Oh yeah." Now that they were actually having a conversation, it gave her an idea. "What's your name?"

He grinned. "Why?"

"I like to know the names of the men I'm having sex with," she said, trying to keep her voice even.

"Call me Sam."

"Sam. Sam and Chuck." She nodded to herself. Those probably weren't their real names, but at least she something to call them. Maybe she could get on their good sides and earn extra favors...

"Okay, I'll give you both blowjobs for a shower, some food and toilet paper."

"Deal. But we get to watch you shower. And you have to let us come in your mouth."

Diane nodded. "Okay."

She heard the cell door unlock and creak open. She stood, expecting to see both Chucky and Sam there. But it was only Sam. Was this the break she was looking for?

Yet something made her wait. She feared another beating. And she doubted she could get the keys away from him anyway. Even if she did and managed to unlock the door at the end of the corridor, Chucky would be waiting. The whole floor was probably monitored.

She stepped out into the cooler corridor and glanced around at the other cells. Did they have shanghaied girls inside as well, forced to perform for their suppers?

A faint voice suddenly caught her attention just as Sam grabbed her arm. She twisted violently out of his grip and ran to a door across the hall.

"Hello! Can you hear me?" She shouted.

"Yes!" the girl's voice was faint. "Help me! I'm Vicki! I'm trapped here!"

Sam grabbed her from behind and snarled, "That will be good for a whipping for the both of you!" He dragged her down the corridor, screaming.

She shut up when Sam slapped her. Still, she had some hope now. *She wasn't alone! Maybe they can work together!* She remembered the girl's name: Vicki. But she hadn't had time to tell her who she was.

Chucky was waiting down the hall. They took her to a tiled bathroom, where every clomp of their boots seemed to echo. Diane was allowed to shower, for which she was grateful. The water felt wonderful and she drank her fill. There was soap and shampoo and she used both extensively, washing her hair twice because she didn't know when she'd have another opportunity.

All the while, the two leering guards stood outside the tiled shower stall and watched her, making cracks about how cute she was and what they wanted to do with her. Diane was helpless to resist.

When she was done, she reached up to turn off the water and Sam said, "Wait."

She paused, one hand on the faucet and turned to look over her shoulder. Sam held up a can of shaving cream and a disposable razor. She raised an eyebrow.

"We want to watch you shave your legs. That always turns Chucky on, you see. As for me, I want to watch you shave your cute little bush."

A stab of new fear went through her. Shave off her pubic hair? The idea made her feel even more vulnerable, if that was possible. Diane knew better than to argue. Her ass still felt the effects of her beating and she guessed she had another one coming for daring to try to contact the girl in the other cell. So she nodded and took the items.

Lathering up, she shaved her legs first, bending over facing them at first as she shaved one leg. But Sam made her turn around to do the other leg, giving them a good shot of her pink ass and the hint of her pussy, peeking through her thighs.

When she was done, she hesitated before shaving her mound.

"Come on, get with it—you don't want to make things worse."

Nodding, she lathered up the strip of hair and gently shaved it, starting at the edges and working in until it was gone. She rinsed off, feeling so completely naked now.

"Wait, let me see if you did a good job," Sam said.

She stood just outside the splash of the shower, her legs apart and allowed the guard to squat down and stare at her most private part of her. When he finally nodded his satisfaction, she felt completely violated.

Diane turned off the shower and Chucky handed her a towel, which she tried to use to cover herself as she dried off. But he yanked it away before she was quite finished, exposing her to their gaze again. At least she felt clean again, she thought.

"Okay, drop to your knees and give Chucky here his blowjob."

"And you'll feed me, afterwards?"

"After you give me mine. That was the deal."

She nodded and dropped to her knees in front of the muscular guard. Chucky wasn't going to help, so she reached out and unbuckled his belt and unzipped his pants. His cock was stubby and only semi-hard, but once she slipped her mouth around it, she could feel it grow inside. David used to like blowjobs, she remembered, and she tried to pretend it was him, back in the old days, when they had been crazy about each other. She licked and sucked and gave him her best technique. Apparently, it worked, for Chucky grasped her head and thrust deep down her throat and she could feel his cock squirting his seed into her esophagus.

She choked and her eyes watered before he let her go. She gasped and bent over, fearing she might throw up. However, her stomach was empty and the feeling passed.

"She's a real good cock-sucker," Chucky informed Sam.

"Good. I'm gonna get mine real soon. Come on, slut."

She rose on shaky legs and followed them back to her cell.

"Chucky, why don't you go fetch Miss Landis here her reward while I get mine," Sam said as he pushed her back into her prison. The other guard nodded and grinned, then headed down the corridor.

Diane found her knees and waited, her hands in her lap. Sam came close and she unbuckled his belt and fished out his cock. It was large and veiny and she wasn't sure she would be able to fit that into her throat. Her eyes went wide.

"Nice, huh?"

She nodded and took the tip into her mouth. He pushed past her tongue and she thought she might choke. Diane had to use both hands to stroke him. Bringing him off took some struggle and she had to use all of her tricks to finally get him to ejaculate. He pulled back and squirted into her mouth, across her face and even in her hair. Sam laughed as he zipped up.

The door slammed, leaving Diane sobbing on her knees by the bed. Then she heard the words she'd been waiting for and scrambled to her feet like an eager puppy.

"Fair's fair," Sam said and thrust a sandwich and a half-roll of toilet paper through the slot.

She grabbed them and retreated to her bed like an animal hoarding her prize. Quickly devouring her sandwich, she sat back against the pillows and contemplated her dismal situation. She noted no one had cleaned out the chemical toilet and her wastes stank up the room. More psychological torture, she assumed.

When the lights came up the next morning, Diane had made up her mind that being forced to give blowjobs to these assholes was simply something she had to do in order to stay alive. She resolved to stop crying about it and just do it. When her father rescued her, then she could see these two men suffer. It wasn't like she'd never given a blowjob before!

When the red light came on and she pushed the button, Diane had convinced herself that it would be all right. The guards showered regularly and they were good about honoring their agreements, so she could survive.

When she heard boot steps, she waited by the door on the bed. The door opened and Sam came in.

"So, slut, you ready to earn your food and water today?"

Sighing, she nodded her acquiescence.

"Good, 'cause we got some visitors who are just dying to see you."

She looked up, startled, to see the cop Darkins and his partner walk in. Both were wearing their uniforms and both had the same lecherous grins on their faces. She was immediately struck by how corrupt this town must be.

"Hey, darlin'," Darkins said. "You remember my partner, Lewis?"

She could only nod, her body otherwise frozen.

"Sam here was tellin' us how good you were at cocksuckin', so we thought we'd get a sample."

Now she shook her head, her plan to accept Sam and Chucky tossed aside. Was she going to have to blow the whole police force?

"Oh, but you pushed the button," Sam pointed out from behind them. "Guess that means you boys get to spank her."

"No! Wait! I'll do it!" The words tore out of her.

"There now, we always like to see a prisoner being cooperative, don't we, Sam?" Darkins said.

Diane felt tears come to her eyes—tears she promised herself she wouldn't shed—as Darkins stepped forward and unzipped his pants. She dropped to her knees in front of him and took his cock into her mouth. He wasn't large and she wanted to make some crack but she knew that would only get her into trouble. She sucked him and teased him for several minutes as the other men watched until he finally squirted into her mouth.

As she knelt there fighting back tears, Lewis got into position. "Hey, honey, don't cry. You'll find my cock ain't nearly as disappointing as Darkins'!" He guffawed and the other two joined in.

She was forced to accept his cock into her mouth and suck him to his satisfying conclusion. When she tasted her second load of sperm of the morning, she realized she was nothing but a whore.

As they left, Chucky appeared to bring her a sandwich and a bottle of water. Then the door was closed with a clang, leaving her alone to cry.

The next morning, Diane woke up to a new horror. She felt that familiar cramping in her stomach and realized she was having her period. Big surprise, she thought, since her birth control pills had been confiscated along with everything else she owned. She noticed she had already stained the sheet with a couple drops of blood so she ran to the toilet and sat on it. After she relieved herself, she wiped up with a few precious sheets of paper, then used another wad to stem her menstrual flow.

She felt ridiculous, holding the pad of paper between her legs. Jesus! Would they make her walk around like this all week? It was humiliating.

When she heard Sam at the door, she noticed the light had not gone on. They must've seen her on the cameras. Diane waddled to the corner of the bed and sat down.

"Hey, honey," he said. "Is Aunt Flow in town? You havin' a bloody mary? Has Scarlett come home to Tara?" He cracked himself up with his jokes.

Diane just sat there, thoroughly shamed and said nothing.

"Well, don't you worry—we'll get you fixed up in no time. How about if I have the doc come visit you?"

Her ears perked up. A doctor? "Yes!" she said at once. "Yes, send the doctor!" Surely she could reason with him! He'd tell these assholes to treat her with some dignity and work to improve her conditions. He might even order her release.

"Okay, honey. Will do." The slot slammed shut.

Diane waited anxiously, one hand between her legs. It seemed to take a long time for the doctor to show up. She had gone through another few pads of toilet paper in the meantime.

When she heard the boots, she raced to the door and waited. When it opened, Sam stepped aside and a tall thin man in a dark suit with a bad combover came through the door, carrying a black bag. Diane was embarrassed and disappointed, all at once. This was her doctor? He looked more like an undertaker. She shrank down, still holding the damn wad of toilet paper against herself.

"There, there, little missy, it's all right," he said and despite his strange appearance, it was the first time someone had been nice to her. She began to cry uncontrollably. The doctor turned to Sam. "What the hell is the meaning of this? Have you no decency?"

Sam stammered, "Well, the sheriff..."

"I don't give a rat's ass what the sheriff says. You can't treat prisoners this way! Just look at her!"

Diane was huddled on the bed, nodding and sobbing. Finally! Someone would rescue her from this nightmare!

"Now, doc, I—"

"And it stinks in here! As a health care professional, I'm ordering you to get this toilet changed! You hear me?"

"Uh, yessir." Sam stepped past them and picked up the smelly toilet. They had to climb on the bed to allow him to pass with it. The door slammed shut, leaving the two of them alone. Diane noticed the slot was also closed, although the guards still had those damn cameras.

"Now, missy? Nothing to be ashamed of, we'll get you fixed up."

"Th-th-they t-t-took m-my c-clothes," she stammered through her tears.

"I know and I'm going to have a talk with Dave, you can bet on that."

She stared at him. "Dave?"

"Oh, that's the sheriff. Dave Robinett."

Diane thought about her own Dave, so far away. For a moment, she wished she had never left him. She wouldn't be in this mess if she hadn't!

The doctor was being so kindly, she felt ashamed for judging him by his looks. He took out a stethoscope and listened to her heart.

"I'm o-o-kay, I just need a tampon," she said, gaining control over her emotions.

"Oh, yes, of course, I'm sorry." He reached into his bag and pulled out a single tampon and handed it over. "I'm sorry, that's all I have right now. I'll talk to the sheriff."

Diane nodded, thankful for this small favor. "Can you excuse me for a moment?"

He nodded and actually turned his back. He was being so kind. She went to the corner where the toilet had been, squatted down and slipped the tampon inside. Using a bit of toilet paper to wipe herself off, she turned to the doctor, feeling like a new woman.

"Oh, thank you doctor! You don't know how it's been here! They had a trial without allowing me to be there! And they added charges that we're true! I never resisted arrest! And now—now they're making me do things...so I can eat and drink. It's not fair!" She found herself babbling and slowed to a stop.

"I know, miss. I'll do what I can. But I'm employed by the sheriff, so I have limited power, you see. I mean, they could just replace me with a doctor who was more, um, amenable to their procedures. You understand?"

"As long as you try, that's all I ask. I mean, this isn't right!"

"One thing I can do is offer you protection, from, you know. Would you like some birth control pills?"

"Yes!" It wasn't what she really wanted—she wanted the doctor to tell her he'd make them leave her alone. In the meantime, this would have to do. "Yes, I'll take those."

"Good." He rummaged in his bag and pulled out the familiar round disc of pills. "Your period started today?"

She nodded.

"Okay, then you know to start these in four days time, all right?"

Diane took the pills, grateful that she was so fortunate. "Oh! There's another girl too—across the hall. I think she's in the same boat as I am. Maybe you could look in on her."

"Very well. I'll talk to them." He looked through the bag. "Now, back to you. I want to give you a vitamin shot."

She started. "A vitamin shot?"

"Yes. You look run-down. I know they haven't been feeding you well. Plus, I'll leave some vitamin pills with the guards. Make sure you take one every day. It will really help you."

Diane nodded, not sure she wanted a shot. But she didn't say anything as the doctor filled a syringe, swabbed her skin and jabbed it into her upper arm.

"Ow!"

"Sorry." He wiped up the area with another cotton ball and put his equipment away. "There, you'll feel better in no time. Just keep up with the pills, okay?"

"Okay." He got up and she grabbed his arm. "Doc! Wait! What about my clothes? Can you get me some clothes? I hate it that they keep me naked her like some kind of animal."

"I'll talk to the sheriff," he said, nodding his head. "I'll come back to check on you later."

He banged on the door and Sam let him out. Diane felt tired, so she returned to her bed and fell across it. For the first time in days, she had hope.

Sam and Chucky came back later, bringing a clean-smelling chemical toilet. Diane expected they would demand a blowjob each, but they seemed remarkably subdued. The doctor must've complained loudly enough for them to stop treating her so wickedly.

As they were about to leave, she asked, "Clothes? The doctor said he'd see about getting me some clothes."

"Oh, yeah." Chucky said, looking dejected. Diane almost smiled.

Sam waited while Chucky left and returned a few minutes later with a sundress she'd never seen before. "Hey, what about my clothes?"

"The ones you had were pretty stinky. We just threw those away. I guess your suitcases are still in impound. We can't get to those. We had this leftover. Don't worry—it's been washed."

She took it and slipped it over her head. It was a bit small, forcing her breasts up against the front and the hem was short, coming to about mid-thigh. But it covered her and Diane treasured it. "Thank you," she said automatically.

"Yeah, well, don't thank us, thank the doc," Sam said and the guards left.

Now we're getting somewhere, she thought.

Diane was surprised the next morning when the red light came on. She thought the doctor had chastised the sheriff's department sufficiently that these little games would stop. She refused to push it. After an hour, she realized she needed a new tampon. Plus she was hungry and thirsty again. Reluctantly, she pushed the button and the green light seemed to mock her.

Sam came by after a while and opened the slot. "What do you need today, m'lady?"

Diane ignored his sarcasm. "I need a new tampon. Plus food and drink."

She'd love another shower but decided not to risk it.

"Well, that's a lot to ask."

A lot to ask? Basic necessities, more like it. "Look," she said evenly. "I thought the doc got through to you guys. You can't treat prisoners like this! You can't make us beg and do, uh, nasty things to earn the things we require to survive. I'll bet if a prisoner ever died from your shenanigans, there'd be hell to pay!"

He shrugged. "Yeah, maybe." He counted on his stubby fingers. "Let's see, tampon, food and drink—that's three items. But there are only two guards on duty. So you're going to have to agree to give someone else a blowjob, the way I'm seein' it."

Diane exploded. "What! The doctor said he'd take care of that. He was going to talk to the sheriff!"

"Oh, he did, he did. And the sheriff is the one you're gonna have to blow now. He was pretty mad, having a prisoner squeal to the doc so she could get special privileges."

She was stunned. Her mouth opened and closed and no sound came out. It made an evil kind of sense—of course the sheriff was crooked. Of course he'd be mad that the doctor scolded him. What was she thinking? The doctor had no power—he even admitted as much! All she had done was stir up a hornet's nest.

"Plus, Dave is going to want to personally administer your punishment, for being such a complainer."

She felt sick. She staggered back and sat on the bed, tears rolling down her cheeks. "Nooo," she said softly. "Nooo."

Diane had no more energy for arguing. First Sam came in, then Chucky and she gave them both blowjobs until her jaw ached and they squirted down her throat. In exchange, she got a single tampon. They told her the sheriff would bring her the food later.

"Don't want you to have a full stomach when he's whipping you," Sam chuckled. "Oh, and one more thing," he said as he stood in the open door. "When the sheriff comes, he's pretty mad. So if you don't want to have the hide whipped right off of you, then you'd better be on your knees and naked when he comes in. Just a word to the wise."

She sat on the cement floor for a long time after they left, her dress stained with her tears, her heart heavy. Her bottom ached and she hadn't even been beaten yet.

Diane inserted the new tampon and rolled the old one up in toilet paper. She realized she was quickly running out and promised herself she'd be more careful.

When she heard boots in the corridor, she stripped off her dress and was on her knees facing the door when the slot opened. Sam's face grinned at her. He turned and spoke to someone she couldn't see.

"Oh, look, our little slut is being very good. She's hoping you'll go easy on her, sheriff." Then he laughed and she heard a deep-bellied laugh next to him. Her heart sank.

The door came open and there, framed in it, stood a large man. He must've stood six-four and probably weighed close to three hundred pounds. He was wearing a linen suit that bulged around the middle. To Diane, he looked like a caricature—Boss Hogg from "The Dukes of Hazzard." He had a fleshy face and dark curly hair. His piggy eyes narrowed when he spotted her.

"So is this our little complainer?" he bellowed. "Don't look like she's complainin' too much right now." He turned over his shoulder to Sam. "In fact, it looks like she's eager to please."

"Oh, she is, Dave, she is. Why she just gave Chucky and me the sweetest blowjobs this side of Meridian!"

"Uh huh." He came closer and she shied back. His stomach bulged out above her head and she felt she was about to be crushed.

"Girl, you in a heap o' trouble."

"Please, sir, I was trying—"

He backhanded her and she let out a yelp and fell against the bed. Before she could recover, he was on her, picking her up like a rag doll and forcing her down on her stomach on the sheet, a massive hand holding her by the neck. It had happened so suddenly, Diane was frozen in place. But when she heard the belt being pulled from his pants, she began to fight, kicking her feet in a useless effort to get free.

"Oooooh-wweee! Looks like we got a fighter on our hands. She felt his hand tighten on her throat, his fingers reaching all the way around her neck. "How 'bout if I just squeeze until you pass out? Would you like that better?"

Diane felt her air cut off and spots formed in front of her eyes. She stopped kicking her legs immediately and lay limply. He let go and she gasped for air.

"Now, another outburst like that and you're gonna wish you hadn't, trust me." She heard him folding the belt in his massive hands and braced herself for the inevitable.

WHACK! She screamed and tried to get up, her ass on fire.

"GET DOWN THERE RIGHT NOW YOU SLUT!" he bellowed and she found herself back on her stomach, her hands still trying to cover her red-hot bottom. "MOVE THOSE HANDS OR I'LL BREAK THEM!"

She pulled them away just as he struck her again. WHACK! WHACK! She screamed and cried and begged to no avail. She fainted at one point and felt a sudden splash of water on her face. She came up sputtering and saw Sam holding a partially full bottle of water.

"You awake now, slut? Good."

WHACK! WHACK! The sheriff was trying to kill her. She pleaded and screamed some more. When he finally stopped, she was exhausted and limp as a rag doll. She felt the bed move as the big man got up.

"Now, you learn your lesson, girl?"

Diane nodded weakly.

"Good. Now I unnerstand the doc gave you some birth control pills?"

She nodded, worried that he would take them away.

"Give them to me. Don't worry, we'll see you take them regular. Wouldn't want you to have a bastard child, now would we? But we have to regulate all prescriptions, you unnerstand, of course."

She got up on trembling legs and found her pills that she had hidden under the mattress. She handed them to the sheriff.

"Good." He passed them to Sam. "Now Sam here will make sure you start taking them regular, along with doc's damned vitamins, every day, okay? We're very fair here." He asked Sam, "When she's supposed to start on these things anyway?"

"I dunno. That was sumtin' between her and the doc."

The sheriff turned back to Diane. "Well?"

"Uh, in four more days."

"Okay, you got that?" Sam nodded. "Don't you fuck this up now—we gots to take care of our prisoners, don't we?"

The guard laughed and nodded his head. Diane sat on the bed, waiting for the next horror that would overtake her.

"Now git down here and give me my blow job. And it had better be the best one you've ever given or I'm going to whip your tits right off your chest." He turned to Sam. "Now, this ain't no peep show. Git."

Sam left so quickly it was as if he had never been there at all.

Despite her aches and pains, she pulled herself from the bed and got down on her knees in front of the sheriff. He unbuckled his pants and she reached in to pull out his enormous cock. It was even larger than Sam's. There was no way she could get that into her throat.

But her ass told her she could do it. She had to. She strained her mouth and managed to get the head inside it. It took both her hands to fit around the girth of his cock. She licked and teased and sucked and rubbed, feeling the desperation driving her forward. Her hands soon ached, her mouth hurt and still she pressed on. After about fifteen minutes, she realized she couldn't do it. She began to sob around his cock.

"That the best you kin do?"

Diane looked up through tear-stained eyes. "I'll try to do better. You're just so big, sir!"

She expected him to be angry, but instead he laughed. "Well, it takes a special woman to tame ol' Whitesnake here."

Diane felt enormous relief. It was short-lived.

He squatted down until his face was closer to hers. He reached out a big hand and cupped her pussy, feeling the string to her tampon between his fingers. "I can see you're on the rag and all, so you're off the hook for now. But when you're all done bleedin', remember this: My cock is going to go up your pussy and you're going to enjoy it. In fact, you're going to become my cock hound. 'Cause if you don't, why, I'm going to whip you just like this every day until you learn to worship my cock."

For a visceral moment, Diane could feel that monster going up into her guts and she shook. "Please, you can't! I'll be killed!"

"Maybe so. Then we'll just bury you in potter's field and that'll be it."

She stared at him. He would to that? Could he do that and get away with it?

"The next time I see you, you'd better be nekkid on the bed with your legs spread and a 'come hither' look on your face, you hear?"

She nodded, all the blood draining from her face. Dizziness threatened to overwhelm her and she gripped the bed to stay upright.

"Good." With effort, he pulled his massive body to his feet and zipped up. "Now I'll call that a decent effort, even though you didn't bring me off. I only know of one lady who could take Whitesnake down her throat and that was after months of practice!" He guffawed and pounded on the door. It opened at once and Sam was there.

"Give the little lady her reward. She tried, that's all a body can ask for."

Sam nodded and brought her a ham sandwich and a bottle of water. After they left, Diane didn't feel like eating for the first time since she'd been imprisoned. She lay the sandwich and water bottle on the bed and looked over her shoulder at her ass. It was bright red and purple and blue. It looked as bad as it felt. It would be a long time before she would be able to sleep on her back.

The next few days ran together for Diane. Every morning, the red light would go on. She'd hit the button. Sam or Chucky would come in and she'd be forced to strip and give him a blowjob. Sometimes it was just one, sometimes both. In exchange, she'd get another tampon and some food and water. And a vitamin pill of course. Sam would always watch her swallow it, telling her, "I gotta report back to the doc that I saw you take it, so down the hatch."

It was about the third day after her visit by the doctor that Diane began to suspect there was something in that pill besides vitamins. For one, it made her feel slightly...odd. Not dizzy or sick or anything obvious. It was more like, slow. Yes, she felt slow, both mentally and physically.

The next day when he came in, she tried to hide it under her tongue. He caught her at it, of course. "Hey, I promised the doc that I'd make you take them. Personally, I think we're just coddling you. You don't need no vitamins—you need a good stiff cock!"

Diane knew her period would end tomorrow and then all hell would break loose, starting with that monster of a sheriff.

"I don't want them," she said. "They make me feel, uh, funny."

"You gotta talk to the doc about that. Meanwhile, swallow."

She swallowed. The threat of another beating always hung over her. Her ass had faded from bright red to purple and yellow, and Diane would do just about anything to avoid another beating.

"Uh, Sam?"

"Yeah?"

"The birth control pills need time to work. I can't just start taking them the same day as…well, you know. Can I see the doc?"

"I'll ask the sheriff. You know, he's not too excited about the last time the doc visited you."

"But I'll tell you what. I can give you the first pill today, if you'd like."

Diane knew that would offer little, if any, protection. But it was better than nothing. She nodded. Sam went and got the pills and watched as she punched one out from the plastic case and popped it into her mouth.

"Okay, I did my part…" He waved his hand at her.

She stripped off the ratty sundress and got down on her knees. She unzipped Sam and took his cock into her mouth. She knew what he liked by now and had him cleaned out and zipped up within five minutes.

Chucky appeared at the door and she took care of him too. He took a bit longer, but only because his cock was large—but not as large as the sheriff's. Afterward, she sat on her haunches and waited for her meal.

When a stranger walked in and Sam told her to "get busy," Diane balked. "Who's he?"

Sam laughed. "Does it really matter? You'll blow him because I tell you to or you don't get to eat."

"But I already gave—"

Sam's hand slapped her casually across the face. It was more of a shock than painful. She looked up at him, eyes already filling with tears.

"Want me to get out my belt?" he asked. He already knew the answer. Diane's ass was far too sore for any further punishment.

Without further protest, Diane unbuckled the stranger's belt and unzipped him. He was short man with reddish hair and she wondered what his relationship was to this twisted sheriff's department. His cock, she was glad to see, was of normal size. She took it inside her mouth and pretended he was a long-lost friend. She had him coming within ten minutes. When he squirted down her throat, she swallowed it quickly and didn't let a drop pass her lips.

He pulled out and zipped up. "You were right, Sam," he said. "She's good."

"Told ya. Now pay up."

Diane watched in horror as the redhead pulled out his wallet and handed Sam ten dollars. He was renting her out!

"How dare you—"

Slap! This time it was Chucky who slapped her. She held her face in her hands, sobbing quietly, until the stranger left.

Sam bent down and pulled her chin up so she could see him. "Listen, cunt. You'll do as we say—it don't matter who you blow or fuck for your supper. We always honor our deals, don't we?"

She nodded, feeling broken inside. "I'm sorry," she whispered.

"That's better." He looked over at Chucky. "Guess you'd better get her lunch."

Chucky left and returned a few moments later with a tampon, a cold fried egg sandwich and another bottle of water. "Here ya go, slut. Enjoy."

Both men laughed as they left her there on the floor, holding her precious food and sobbing.

Diane felt strangely detached about what would happen the next day. Her period was almost over and everyone knew it. That sheriff would be in here first thing to rip her apart. But somehow, she couldn't muster up the fear she had felt earlier. Was she getting used to this horrible place?

Her stomach growled. This practice of one sandwich a day wasn't doing her any good. She guessed she had lost about ten pounds already and she had only weighed one-thirty when she had driven into this god-forsaken county. At this rate, she'll be a skeleton in ninety days. Diane tried to calculate how many days left and got confused. Her mind was so easily confused now.

She slept on and off that afternoon, for there was nothing else to do. When the lights dimmed, she felt all slept out but managed to fall into a troubled slumber anyway, her sundress still wrapped around her body.

The next day she felt hollow and smelly. Hair had grown back in her underarms and pussy and she knew Sam didn't like that. Maybe he'd let her shower before...She wrinkled her brow. Oh, yes, Before the sheriff came in and fucked her.

She giggled. Fucked her. David used to fuck me, she thought. I liked it. I'm not too sure about the sheriff, though. His cock was the largest she'd ever seen. It was like a whitesnake, she mused. Wasn't there a band by that name?

The door rattled and she sat up. "Oh, gotta pee," she said to no one in particular and jumped onto the pot. Sam came in as she was noisily voiding herself, her sundress up around her waist.

"Jeez, warn a fella." He seemed to be in a good mood. He had a digital camera in one hand.

She wiped herself off. "I'm almost out of toilet paper," she said. "See?"

"Yeah, we'll take care of that. First things first. You stink. You ready to earn a shower today?"

"Oh, yes!" She stood up and swept her dress off over her head. "And my pussy is all hairy too."

"It certainly is!" He led her without touching her to the bathroom. "Go ahead. I'll sit out here." He found a folding chair and sat heavily on it.

Diane loved the showers. She spent a half-hour in there, washing and singing softly to herself. She was startled by the flash a few times, but quickly got used to it. When Sam tossed her the razor and the shaving cream, she got right to work, starting with her legs and working to her underarms. When she began shaving her stubbly mound, Sam took a lot of pictures, and she giggled. It seemed very funny to her.

After she had dried off, he took her back to her cell. Chucky was waiting and she stepped inside, turned around and dropped to her knees. Before Sam could approach her, she wrinkled her nose. "It stinks in here," she said. She turned and saw her sundress on the bed. "Eww, it's this. Can you wash it for me?"

"Sure, honey," Sam said, taking it. He tossed it outside the cell. "Now get busy."

She made love to his cock, just the way he liked it. She didn't want to get him off quickly today, so she slowed down when he was close in order to prolong the moment. When he finally exploded into her throat, her lips mashed tightly against his pubic bone, he really came a lot, she could tell. He pulled out and she felt an odd sense of pride.

"Wow, that was the best yet! You're really become quite a good cock sucker!"

Diane blushed.

"My turn," Chucky said, coming in. Sam zipped up and stepped out. He didn't close the door.

As usual, Chucky proved to be more challenging but Diane rose to it. She managed to get most of his cock down her throat. For some reason, her body felt more relaxed today and she didn't choke as much. He grabbed her head like he usually did, and she didn't feel that sense of panic. He pounded her throat, his hand gripping her tightly and she just hung on until he erupted inside her.

When he pulled her away, she took a shuddering breath but didn't choke. Some of his seed spilled onto her naked breasts and she quickly scooped it up and swallowed it.

"Wow! Oh, wow! I see what you mean, Sam! She's great now!"

"Wait 'til Dave hears about this!"

Diane sat there, only half listening to them.

"Oh! Almost forgot. Your pills, ma'am." Sam was sure being nice today.

He handed her a vitamin pill and a birth control pill and she popped them into her mouth. He handed her a bottle of water and she washed them down. She waited for her sandwich and was told, "The sheriff wants to fuck you first."

"Oh," she said. For some reason, that seemed perfectly normal.

The guards left, leaving the door ajar. That was odd. It had never happened before. She went to it and peaked through the opening. The corridor appeared to be empty. She pushed the door open a little more and peered around it. The two guards had gone, all right.

Diane didn't know what to do. Should she try to escape? That seemed impossible. There were locked doors at the end of the hall. A thought burrowed its way into her brain. The other girl! She slipped out of the cell and padded naked to the one across the corridor. Tapping on it, she asked quietly, "Hello? Anyone there?"

Silence.

"Hello?" She tapped harder now.

Nothing.

Then she almost laughed at herself. "You can peek through the slot, silly!" She reached up and undid the latch and slid it open. She had to pull herself up to peer over the lip.

The cell was empty.

"Well, it just means she's been released. She served her time," she said in a whisper.

Diane slid back down and looked around the hallway. There were two other cells and she checked them both. They were also empty. She returned to her cell, fearing she might get caught and punished. Her butt was still a little sore. She looked back and could see the purple had mostly faded to red and orange.

She was on her bed when she heard the heavy tramp of the men returning. The sheriff's massive body appeared in the doorway. She shrank back—and he did something unexpected. He smiled.

"Well, hello, little lady. How are you today?"

"Fine, sir," she squeaked.

"Good! That's real good." He approached and stopped to look over his shoulder. "Now you boys git," he said. She saw Sam and Chucky ease the door closed and heard their footsteps echo down the corridor. Now it was just her and him. Her pussy twitched.

He came close and put a massive paw up against her jawline. "I hear you've been real good lately."

"Yessir." She wasn't sure what he meant but she was certainly going to agree with him!

"Good. Now, you know why I'm here, right?"

She looked down. "Yessir."

"Don't you fret too much. I know I'm big, but a girl like you should be able to handle him just fine. All you gotta do is relax."

"I'll try, sir."

"Good. Now let's start with one of your special blowjobs. Don't worry if you can't get it all in, I just want to see you do your best."

Diane dropped to her knees and unzipped him. Whitesnake was just as massive as she remembered him. She giggled.

"Whatcha laughin' at girl?" His voice had an edge to it.

"I just started calling it Whitesnake in my head when I saw it, just like you do."

He laughed, throwing his head back. "Why, that's good. I like to hear you call it by name. We'll do that from now on, okay?"

"Okay." She hefted the semi-hard cock with both hands. "And okay to you too, Mr. Whitesnake."

She began to lick it from balls to tip, feeling it grow in her hands. She could get the tip inside her mouth, but little else. She tried to massage him and his cock felt like an anaconda in her tiny hands. She worked on Whitesnake for several minutes and had made him reach a full erection, but she couldn't make him come.

"I'm sorry," she said in a small voice, fearing he might whip her again.

"Don't worry, little girl, just climb up on that bed."

At that moment, she remembered what he had ordered her to do, so she lay on her back, put her legs wide apart and crooked her finger at him. She hoped she had the right expression on her face.

He laughed again and crawled up over her. He smelled vaguely of cigars and sweat, but she didn't care. All of her attention was focused on Whitesnake. He laid it on her bare stomach and told her to prepare herself.

"What do you mean? Tell me what to do."

"That's right—you just listen to me and you'll be fine. Just start rubbing it against your cute cunt."

She did as he asked and she felt her cunt grow very wet. All of her attention was concentrated on that cocktip, rubbing, rubbing, rubbing, driving her crazy.

"Ohhh," she moaned.

"You like that?"

"Yes, it feels goooood."

"Go ahead and see if you can just get the tip in, a little bit."

Diane liked being in control of Whitesnake. She grabbed it with both hands and helped steer it into her. Her eyes widened when the tip spread her lips apart and popped in.

"Ohhh, wow," she said. "It's big."

"I know. Just take your time, sweetie." He nibbled on her nipples, making her squirm with delight.

She pulled it in and pushed it out and the sheriff helped her.

It was so big! She couldn't possibly take that whole thing inside her. Could she?

Her mouth opened wider, as if that might make it easier. She imagined her pussy spreading as wide as her jaw so he could fit more of Whitesnake inside her velvety tunnel.

Dave became bolder now, pushing harder, even when she wasn't ready.

"Oh! Oh!"

Her hands now sought to hold it back for it seemed destined to fit its entire length inside her. Her hips cracked as she pulled them wide apart. He pressed harder.

"Careful now. Easy. Slow, go slow."

Her words had little effect on him. His cock was being thrust into her, whether she was ready or not. He pulled back, giving her a small respite, and pressed forward again. Soon he had a rhythm going: Forward hard, back a little, forward hard again. Diane could feel her pussy lubricating desperately, trying to make the monster's passage easier.

And then a strange thing happened. Just when she was sure she couldn't possibly fit Whitesnake in her, her pussy began to tingle in an usual way. Heat spread through her loins, up through her stomach and into her chest. Her mouth opened wider and her breath came in short gasps.

"Oh! Oh! Oh! Oh!"

And the cock slipped through her fingers and disappeared inside her. "Oh my god!"

"That's it, baby. I knew you could do it," he said, his voice tight.

He pulled back and slid it right up inside again. It didn't hurt this time.

"It doesn't hurt!" she blurted.

"Good. Now just lay back and enjoy the ride."

He moved back and forth, starting slow and speeding up. Diane felt her body move up with each in-stroke until her head was jammed against the pillows. A warm fire spread throughout her body and she thought she might faint.

"Oh my god! Oh my god! Oh my god!"

And there it was, on the horizon, something she never thought she could achieve with this monster inside her—an orgasm. It came rushing at her, faster and faster and she began pressing back against him, driving his cock deeper into her until she could tell when it pushed past her cervix and entered her womb itself.

God! No one had ever fucked her like this. Ever.

"Fuck me, oh yes, fuck me, fuck me." She was babbling and wasn't aware of it.

She could sense that the sheriff was close now for his mouth came open and he started to make odd noises in his throat.

"Yeah, baby, yeah, baby," she cooed, encouraging him. She held back her orgasm for as long as she could and just when it overwhelmed her and her mind was swept away, she felt the cock inside her erupt, spewing its heavy load deep within her womb.

"Oh my god! OH MY GOD!" She shrieked with the power of their mutual climax and fainted dead away.

When she came to, Dave was sitting on the edge of the bed, a smile on his face. She managed to sit up and saw a huge puddle of goo between her legs and spreading across the sheet.

"Oh, jeez—how long was I out?"

"Just a couple of minutes. I didn't want to wake you; you looked so peaceful."

"Peaceful! More like knocked out. I've never had a cock like yours before."

"Well, we can fix that." He got up.

Diane felt suddenly alone. "Wait. Do you have to go?"

He smiled. "Missin' me already, little girl?" He leaned down and kissed her left breast. "Don't worry—I'll be back."

He adjusted his pants and hit the door with a fist. It opened at once and he breezed out past Sam.

"How was it, sheriff," she heard Sam say.

The sheriff's words were lost when the door clanged shut, leaving her alone once again.

Everything changed from that point on. There were no more lights and "trades" for food or water. Diane was made comfortable—as comfortable as one could be in a jail cell. She was given food and water whenever she asked for it. Her toilet was changed frequently. They gave her plenty of toilet paper. She even got a new sundress, one that fit her a little better.

And every morning, the men would line up. Sam and Chucky. The town mayor. The occasional strangers. And, of course, the sheriff.

They all fucked her silly, making her come again and again.

The first time the doctor fucked her, she'd been surprised. She didn't think he would do that to her, a man of medicine and all. But it sure felt good. She giggled when she first saw his cock—it was long and thin, just like he was tall and thin. But she sucked him hard and let him slip it inside. He fucked her like a rabbit and came within a minute.

Of all her lovers, she liked the sheriff a lot—his cock was big, like riding a train into the mountains. It was a long, strenuous ride and she always reached her destination. But Sam's lovemaking was the best. His cock was just the right size and hit all the right places inside her. Whenever he fucked her, she would grab his neck and hang on for dear life, achieving orgasm after orgasm.

She never told the sheriff that Sam was a better lover. She knew better than that!

After a while, they took Diane out of her cell for long periods of time. Once they tied her on her stomach to a table in the break room and she felt many hands on her back and many cocks in her pussy. She must've come a dozen times or more while she was there. Someone had placed a bucket on the floor between her legs and whenever she had to pee, she just let it go, listening to it splash into the bucket. For some reason, it seemed to amuse whoever was in the room, for they always cheered.

One cop wanted to fuck her up the ass and she screamed and cried until he managed to get his cock inside her. Then she settled down and let him have his way with her. After that, many men took advantage of this new hole. There was always a tube of lubricant on the table beside her.

She became a regular visitor to the mayor's office, a short fat man named Jones. He preferred blow jobs, of which by now she was an expert. He liked sticking her under his desk and letting her fondle his cock while he took care of city business.

Another time, she was put under the desk of a rookie cop. The poor kid hadn't been warned so he jumped a mile when he first saw the naked girl crouched under his desk. A note left for him told him if he didn't come in her mouth twice, she would be whipped and they'd make him watch.

He managed to keep her from being whipped that day.

For the next few weeks, someone would take Diane back to her cell at night to rest, but after a certain point, there was no need. She had no plans to escape. She had no concept of escape. She was simply a fuck toy, willing to do whatever men wanted to do with her.

The sheriff took her home with him one night, handcuffed naked in the front seat, her tits thrust out in front of her. He fondled her all the way home, making her horny all over again. He hadn't fucked her that day and she was looking forward to another visit from Whitesnake.

When he pulled into his garage and hauled her inside his home, she was stunned to see a woman in the kitchen. She was a tall redhead, wearing a little too much makeup. She wore a silk robe with dragons and flowers on it. When she saw Diane, she paused, looking her over with one hand on her hip.

"Hi, Dave. So this is the new slut, huh?"

The sheriff patted Diane's naked bottom and said, "You betcha, Sue. She's a peach, isn't she?"

"She sure is. You got her all broken in now?"

"She's as docile as a kitten, aren't ya, slut?"

Diane nodded. "Yessir."

"Well, I can't wait. Bring her into the living room."

Diane was given a gentle push and she followed Sue to a couch, where she was placed on her stomach, her hands still cuffed behind her. Sue lay facing her at one end and opened her legs to either side of the helpless girl. Her robe fell apart, exposing her naked pussy, covered in a fine dusting of curly red hair. Dave sat in a chair nearby and watched.

Sue pointed at her crotch.

"Get busy."

Diane had never pleasured a woman before, but she knew orders when she heard them. She scooted forward on her belly until her tongue could reach the woman's slit and began to lick her.

"Oh, that's good. Now, up, lick up. Now back. Come on, pretend it's your pussy. That's better." With some encouragement, Sue soon had Diane led her to a soul-wrenching orgasm.

"Oh, yes, oh, my, that was good," she said, holding Diane's head against her pussy as she came down from her high. "Now, do it again."

Three orgasms later, Diane was finally pulled free, her face a mess of fluids. Sue dragged Diane off the couch to where her husband was sitting, his huge cock hard in his hands.

With Sue's help, Diane was placed over his jutting cock and made to squat down on it. This surprised her. Why would the sheriff's wife be so eager to have him fuck another woman?

Her thoughts were lost a moment later when the huge head began to plow into her. By this time in her imprisonment, Diane had actually grown accustomed to his cock and it was quickly seated deep within her, her thighs on his.

Sue slapped Diane's ass, making her jump up. When she came down again, she slapped it again. She soon got into a rhythm of fucking herself on the sheriff's cock, with much encouragement from Sue.

When he at last bellowed and came inside her, Diane felt her own orgasm erupt and they shook with pleasure. His seed leaked out around her pussy and soon made a mess of his pants. Sue helped Diane off and she was made to clean up his cock.

Later, they all rested on the couch, satisfied expressions on their faces.

"So you like my husband's monster cock, do ya?" Sue asked her.

"Uh, yeah, but..."

"But what?"

"Aren't you jealous? I mean..."

She laughed. "Nah. When you're married to that monster, you like having someone else around to handle it once in a while. If it was just me all the time, why he'd break me like a piñata."

Diane thought about that, but it just made her head hurt, so she curled up between them and drifted off. Later, she was carried into their king-sized bed. In the morning, she was made to eat Sue's pussy again and later she watched as Dave fucked her like a rag doll.

No one told Diane when ninety days was up. She forgot to ask. Instead of a short-term event in her life, this became her life. She spent most of her time in the sheriff's office or Mayor Jones's office. Rarely did she wear clothes. After a while, people stopped talking to her. She would be brought out and put into position, sometimes tied, sometimes just told to stay. She'd feel a slap on her ass that indicated she should present herself for a fucking. A high slap meant ass, a lower slap to her thighs meant pussy. She'd tip her hips the right way to accommodate them. A slap to her shoulder or face meant suck a cock.

Women came over as well. Sue was a regular visitor, although Dave didn't like seeing his wife climax in front of the men, so Sue would take Diane back to her old cell. They'd come back and Sue would have that glow and Diane's face would be smeared with pussy juice. It was quite amusing to the men.

***

Dave Robinett met Hiram Sands, the junkman, at his lot one afternoon. Hiram showed him a pile of car parts.

"That all that's left of her car?"

"Yep. All the parts with VIN numbers. I sold the rest online."

"Good. You melting that shit down?"

"Oh, yeah. Won't bring much as scrap, o'course."

"That's all right. You know the drill."

"Yeah."

"What about the other girl's car? You know, your girlfriend's."

"Oh, that's stuff's long gone now."

"Good. How much we get?"

"So far, both cars?"

"Yeah."

"Twenty-six hunnert."

"Okay, when you sell the rest, I'll expect my percentage."

"Oh, sure Dave, no problem."

Dave started to walk away, then paused. "Can I see her?"

"Who, Vicki?"

"Yeah. I want to make sure you ain't mistreating her."

Hiram looked uneasy. "Yeah, well, she's all right."

"I want to see her."

"Okay, okay, keep your shirt on."

He led the sheriff to another building at the edge of the junkyard. A line of men snaked out the door. Hiram and the sheriff pushed past them and into the darkened building.

A woman lay tied to a padded sawhorse. Another sawhorse propped up her torso. A man was fucking her. When he came, he pulled out and left by a side door and another man took her place, this time in front. She ovaled her lips around his cock. Dave could see a partner of Hiram's collecting money from the men in line. He'd go down the row. "Blow job? Fuck? Ass or pussy?"

"Jeez, Hiram, you're gonna kill her."

"Ah, no. She likes it."

Dave had to admit, Vicki seemed to have a half smile on her

face most of the time, even as she sucked the spunk from the man in her mouth.

"Wait a minute—how much of that shit did doc give her?"

Hiram looked nervous. "Well, she was regressing somehow. She started to give me some lip, so I had doc increase her dose. I don't know what all he did. Ask him."

"Is this really what you wanted when you begged me to let you have one?"

"Well, I can fuck her any time I want. But I kinda like the money better."

Dave nodded. "You're gonna have to put a limit on her. You don't want to have her fucked to death, now do ya? You know if you do, you won't get another one."

"Aw, man, okay. I'll watch it."

"Good, see that you do. Sluts don't grow on trees, you know."

They both laughed and Dave made his way back to his patrol car and headed home. On the way, he got a radio call from Deputy Darkins.

"Sheriff?"

"Yeah, Frank, go ahead."

"I think we got ourselves another one. A cute redhead. I know you like redheads."

"Great. Take her to the jail, drop her car off at Hiram's. You know the drill."

"I surely do, Dave, I surely do."

TIED & BRANDED

CHAPTER ONE

Bessie lay on her side in the grass, grateful for the shade of the barn this time of day. Time had no meaning any longer; she measured her life by the sun and her twice-daily milkings. Her naked body was tanned dark brown, where it wasn't caked with dirt or dyed with ink. The B in a circle stood out on her right buttock, burned into her flesh. Her brown hair had been cropped close on her head.

Though she was a large woman, her breasts seemed out of place on her chest. They hung down like two ripe watermelons over her swelling stomach, which is why she preferred to lie down whenever possible. Right now, they were especially distended—it was almost time for her afternoon milking. Just the thought of it make her nipples extend and her loins ache with desire, mixed with anxiety.

As if on cue, she heard the clanging of the iron triangle in the barn. She struggled to her hands and knees and began crawling back to the barn. The cowbell around her neck rang, announcing her approach. Her breasts hung down painfully, but there was nothing to be done about it. She could remember a time when she would stand and walk, but those days were long past now. She had learned.

Her Master stood by the gate, smiling down at her. "Come on, Bessie, hurry up," he chided her, slapping her gently with the long, stiff dressage whip he carried in his right hand. She hustled so she wouldn't present such an easy target to him. Her bell clanged louder.

She paused to allow him to clip the lead to the ring in her nose. It was a heavy steel ring that covered most of her upper lip. She disliked it, but at least it no longer hurt—except when he tugged on it too hard.

He led her into the barn, Bessie hurrying to keep up. The structure, a large rectangle, had been divided in two equal rooms. In the first half was where Bessie spent her evenings, chained up in a stall full of hay and old blankets she could use to ward off the chill. When she had first arrived, she had spent all her time here, until she had progressed. They passed by the small milking machine that she no longer used.

Master led her through the double doors into the back section, where the newer milking machine sat in its heavy wooden frame, waiting for her like a promise and a curse. She desperately needed to have her milk drained, yet she knew there would be punishments and pain here too. Still, it was not for her to complain, just to do as ordered.

"Come on, get into position, you know the drill."

Bessie climbed up into the machine, snuggling her hips up against the padded brace and holding onto wooden dowels with both hands as she got into a bicycle position. Her hips were forced up high, so her back was at a slight downward angle toward her head. Her chin rested on another padded brace that held her head up, looking right into the lens of a video camera. The display had been turned around so she could see her face in the small LCD screen. She could hardly recognize herself—her cheeks and jowls seemed puffy and she wondered how much weight she had gained in the last few months. Just beyond the camera was a large, flat-screen monitor, mounted onto a post. It was dark for now.

Once she was in place, she looked down to see the leather boots that were attached to the frame at the base and began to slide her feet inside, forcing her legs wide apart. The boots were covered on the inside with sheepskin, so they fitted softly and snugly around her feet. When both feet were secure, she turned her attention to her hands. Just below the dowels she was gripping, two thick leather gloves were screwed to the sides of the frame. She slipped her hands inside and waited.

"Good girl," Master said. He stepped forward and began to buckle leather straps at the tops of the boots and gloves. Now she was trapped, her ass up, legs apart, pussy exposed. She sighed and settled in. Her breasts, hanging free, ached so.

Master slipped a bucket into a bracket between her legs, then took another camera and put it into position just below her stomach, pointing up at an angle toward her crotch. Bessie used to be embarrassed with the knowledge that he filmed everything, but no more. Now she just waited, for the best part was coming. He moved up to her breasts, her sensitive, aching breasts, and began to wash them gently, removing the dust and dirt. Her breasts were always the cleanest part of her body. After he toweled her off, he massaged her nipples, causing the milk to let down. Fat drops spattered on the ground.

"Ahhh," she groaned, seeing her expression of bliss in the camera display.

Master then began putting the salve onto her breasts, working the soothing agent into her nipples, making them slippery and extended. Bessie groaned again and felt the wetness leak from her open pussy. When he was satisfied her teats were ready, he flipped on the first motor and brought up the milking cups. They attached by suction, so he waited until the vacuum had built up sufficiently, holding them against her breasts until they attached themselves. Bessie groaned a third time as she felt her nipples being sucked down into the milking apparatus at the bottom of each cup.

"Feels good, doesn't it?"

She only nodded. She knew better than to speak.

Master came forward with a tall glass of water, mixed with electrolytes to help her milk production. He used a funnel with a short length of tubing to help her, feeding the end into her mouth. He began pouring the mixture in slowly. She drank it all down, making sure she didn't spill any. She hoped she could control her bladder this time. He gave her so much to drink, it wasn't always possible.

He flipped another switch and she felt the small finger-like kneaders go to work on her nipples—first the left, then the right, then the left again. Her milk began to flow. "Aaaahhhh," she moaned, happy to be relieving her tender breasts at last. The faint sound of her milk being sucked into a container reached her ears. She could feel the wetness increase between her legs.

Master moved into her field of vision, carrying a third camera. She gave him a sideways glance and a thin grin. He smiled and panned along her body until he reached her wide ass. She knew he was zooming in on her gaping pussy, but she didn't care. Her breasts were all that mattered now. Having her nipples massaged like this was heaven.

"Looks like you're stretched out enough, finally," he said, touching that private part of her, testing her wetness. She jumped at his touch, as she always did. Master gave her a little slap on the rump. He moved backward to her side, keeping her in the frame, and put the camera onto a tripod.

She waited while Master went to the back of the barn and called outside. "Come on, Bull! She's all ready for ya!"

She shivered and her mind flew back—was it just four months ago?—to how circumstances had led her to this strange new life. She knew she was mostly to blame, for she had been curious. Too curious. But now her life was no longer her own. Master controlled her fate. She was his milk cow. The funny part of it was, this had once been a fantasy of hers, back when she still thought of herself as Brenda.

***

If a girlfriend had ever set Brenda Wallinsky up on a blind date, she would have told the man about her wonderful personality. In other words, Brenda was no beauty. She was a plain, big-boned Alabama woman of twenty-eight who had rarely dated in her life and doubted she ever would marry. Men hardly ever looked twice at her.

In this absence of romance, she had begun to entertain fantasies. Some were harmless, such as being kidnapped by pirates and being taken away to a secret island. Or having a makeover and waking up to a new life.

But one fantasy in particular kept creeping into her consciousness despite how strange it had seemed. She realized it was a long-suppressed childhood desire and she tried to push it away at first. But it would not be denied and it excited her in a way she could not explain. In her fantasy, she was being milked, her large breasts being squeezed in the hands of a strong man or a machine. A few minutes imaging this when she lay in her bed and her hand would wind up between her legs to bring herself to a powerful orgasm.

Her feelings about being milked originally had taken shape not long after her breasts began to develop when she was twelve. Like her mother, Brenda had large breasts that had embarrassed her as a young girl. Her mother, trying to be helpful, explained that they were large because her babies would, one day, need a lot of milk and she would be able to provide for them easily. She cheerfully described the facts of life to the young girl, making it sound like a noble cause.

"I know you look with envy at those small-breasted girls you see at school every day," her mother had said. "But when they grow up, they'll have to feed their babies from a bottle. You won't. You'll be a better mother to your kids."

Her mother knew what she was talking about due to her involvement in Le Leche League, a group of mothers who advocated breast-feeding over the bottle. She told Brenda that breast milk contained valuable minerals and enzymes that protected the babies and how nursing helped bond the mother and child together. Yet for Brenda, it was the budding sexual feelings she experienced when she thought about it that aroused her young imagination. She began to feel better about her breasts after that and tried to ignore the taunts of her school mates.

It was a field trip her class took to a dairy farm when she was fourteen that cemented her fascination with the entire milking process. It had surprised her how turned on she had been by the sight of the cows being milked, either by hand or machine. She watched carefully as the farmer gently squeezed the cow's teats, squirting a line of milk into the bucket, the sound—szzz, szzz—making her wet between the legs.

Next, the farmer showed how the automatic milkers fitted over the cow's teats. She felt a buzzing in her head and her nipples seemed to stretch themselves out against her bra. She had to turn away for fear that someone would notice, her legs squeezed together tightly.

God, she imagined she could have an orgasm just standing there watching! She had to pinch the soft flesh between her thumb and forefinger until the pain overcame the erotic sensations coursing through her loins. She wondered if something was wrong with her.

On the bus back, the other girls in the class laughed at the poor dumb cows and no one seemed to make the connection between udders and their own breasts, except Brenda. She wisely kept silent.

Alone in her bedroom that night, Brenda allowed her thoughts to return to the barn. She would play with her nipples and imagine she was being milked like the cows she had watched. How would it feel? She instinctively knew she would be a good milker. Just like her mother. While one hand was kept busy stroking her extended nipples, the other drifted down to her pussy. She couldn't believe how wet she was! It took just a few strokes for her to climax into a shuddering orgasm. Her other hand kept pinching her nipples, extending the feeling.

It felt so good she did it again. And again.

Later, she had a dream. Instead of a big black and white dairy cow, Brenda herself was being led into the milking stall. She was naked. The class stood around silently as the farmer made her get down on all fours so he could hook up her breasts to the machine. For some reason, she didn't feel embarrassed to be exposed in front of them. They watched her with wide-open eyes as if she were helping them learn a valuable lesson.

In her dream, her nipples weren't small—they were thick and fat as her finger, so they easily fit into the apparatus. When he turned it on and she felt that sucking, she climaxed in her sleep. She woke up, panting, realizing she had had several orgasms in the last twenty-four hours just thinking about being milked. That dream stuck with her for years and she relived it many times with her fingers.

***

When she turned nineteen, she moved out of her home. Her mother could not afford to send her to college without a hefty scholarship and Brenda's grades hadn't been good enough to win one, so she went right to work. She got a low-paying job as a nurse's aide at a local hospital. Brenda toiled at a few wards for several years before landing her dream job: working at the maternity ward. It was heaven to her. She could educate the new mothers about the benefits of breastfeeding, while secretly getting aroused whenever she watched them. Brenda got that same tingle in her breasts, as if it were she who was holding the baby close, allowing it to suckle on the teat. More than once, Brenda had to retreat to the women's bathroom and masturbate quickly in order to alleviate the built up sexual heat.

Her breasts were more sensitive sex organs than her clitoris, she came to realize. She could come in an instant if her breasts were stimulated first. When she was home alone in her apartment, she often spent several long minutes massaging her breasts before her hand ever touched her clit. And it usually only took a touch to send her over the edge.

Brenda tried to be satisfied with her life, but she wasn't. Because men paid her no attention, she found herself thinking more and more about her strange sexual fetish. She longed to feel those milking cups on her nipples as she had dreamed. Once, she even bought a breast pump, hoping to simulate lactation. It didn't work, of course. Without a baby in her belly, she had no milk. She knew she could take drugs to stimulate her breasts, but feared doing it on her own.

Brenda saved up enough money to buy a laptop and began to explore her unique fetish online. Surely there must be others like herself who might help her understand her strange fixation. Maybe they could "cure" her, although she wasn't sure she wanted to be cured.

The research had the opposite effect, as it turned out. Instead of being advised on how to overcome her fetish, she learned just how many people embraced it. Suddenly, she no longer felt like a freak who had to hide her dark secret. There were other women who not only agreed with her, they encouraged her. They even had a chat room devoted to the subject.

Emboldened, over time Brenda became one of the leaders of the group. Her knowledge of Le Leche League and other breast-related information she had learned as a nurse's aide straightened out many a novice and set the facts out for everyone to see. Instead of being ashamed, she came to realize that she was actually quite normal. She believed she would make a great mother.

Sadly, her plain looks and heavyset frame prevented her from every being attractive enough to the kind of men she liked. And she had no desire to simply use a man to get pregnant—she had seen too many single mothers at the maternity ward who had worried how they might raise a baby on their own. Though she liked the idea of motherhood, what she really wanted was to give milk—at least for now. Babies could come later.

So she turned inward, and began thinking more about how it might feel to be treated like a cow. To be milked by one of those machines. Brenda figured she'd never go beyond the fantasy stage—until she met Jack.

Jack—he gave no last name—was a newcomer to the chat room. He was distant, but polite and joined in during several conversations. It seemed odd to have a man appear to be so knowledgeable about women's breasts, but he did not come across as arrogant or perverted. At first, she was suspicious of him, but he said something one day that sent the heartstrings aflutter.

He had been talking about the best producers of milk and he stated: "The truth is, the skinny model types one sees on TV are the worst for our infants. The true mothers are the ones who carry a little extra weight and have large breasts. And I don't mean fake ones."

Brenda fell a little bit in love with him right then. She responded, congratulating him on his viewpoint and telling him how rare and refreshing it was. Too many men were hung up on body shape, she wrote. She was testing him to see how he might feel about oversized women. He wrote back and assured her that he preferred a full-figured woman with large breasts.

They began a conversation that lasted for several months. At first, she had been embarrassed to describe herself or send photos, despite his support of the larger female form. Finally, after many long conversations that caused her to feel she had found her soulmate, she agreed to send him a photo. She found a flattering one of her in her nurse's aide uniform and emailed it to him.

She cringed afterwards, waiting to hear his dismissive reply. Instead, he had said she had the "perfect" shape to be a wonderful milk producer. Brenda had to sign off almost immediately and bring herself to a massive orgasm.

When she came back on, she asked Jack how he knew so much about milk production and woman's breasts. His reply shocked her. "I run a small farm, dedicated to producing milk for infants whose mothers cannot or will not produce it themselves," he replied. "I sell it to hospitals and home health care agencies."

My god, she thought. What a wonderful man! And a second thought crept in. Could she be one of those women who produce milk for the babies? She asked him about it and was greatly encouraged by his answer.

"I find, through the application of certain safe hormones, I'm able to help even non-pregnant women achieve good milk production."

Brenda was hooked. All that remained were the details.

CHAPTER TWO

She had arrived at Jack's southern Indiana farm on a sunny day in early June. Brenda had been very nervous, feeling that somehow he would reject her. But he welcomed her warmly, giving her a big hug like an old friend. He was a large, ruggedly handsome man, well over six feet, with full head of brown hair slowly going gray. She guessed his age at the early fifties. He had a gentle face and laughed easily, which put her at ease at once.

He showed her around. Inside the farmhouse, there was a room devoted to the lactating women who used mechanical breast pumps he had designed to expel their milk. They came in once every day or so to produce the milk and left to go back to their husbands or boyfriends.

It was an efficient, professional set-up that was run without the hint of sexual pandering. The women discreetly handled the pumps themselves or with the help of a female nurse and Jack never entered the room while they were lactating. The milk was packaged and stored in refrigerators and picked up daily by a small van.

Brenda had been vaguely disappointed. She had fantasized that she might see women milked like cows, such as she had observed on the dairy farm, or had dreamed about. But she kept her mouth shut. Jack was simply performing a valuable public service, after all. What has she been thinking?

Her original plan had been to sign up for the program that would allow her to produce milk. After the tour, she wasn't so sure. She had been embarrassed to tell Jack that she had no place to live locally. She had assumed she would live with him on the farm and perhaps they would even fall in love. She realized he simply wanted a business arrangement, like the other women. She had no friends or family nearby and therefore no support group to rely on while she found a place to live and other employment. After all, producing milk was a part-time job at best.

"I'm sorry, I made a mistake," she told him at the end of her visit, her eyes averted in embarrassment, feeling hot tears burn her eyes. "I thought, foolishly, that the women lived here. I didn't realize that this was to be strictly a part-time endeavor. I-I don't have any place to go right now."

"Actually, I wanted to talk to you about that," he replied. "Remember, we've been talking for months. I feel I've gotten to know you pretty well. I could read between the lines of what you were saying and I wanted to tell you, I feel the same way. You see, I've been looking for someone like you all my life. Someone who wanted to more than just give milk and go home, like these other women. I've been experimenting with new technologies and equipment, you see, trying to better automate the milking experience."

"I'm not sure I understand," she said, her hopes rising.

"Well, I'm a little embarrassed to say it, but I've been modifying equipment used in dairy operations for use with humans. So I guess you could say I'm looking for a woman who wants to explore the idea of being, uh, professionally milked—even if just on a trial basis."

His words elated Brenda. She had been hoping for the same thing, but had dared not mention it aloud for fear of being branded a freak. Her pussy gushed with desire, even at the thought of it.

"And this equipment, has it been tested?" she asked.

"Yes, on a limited basis. I believe it's perfectly safe. But it's never been tested formally and that is the next step."

Brenda knew at once that she wanted to be the one to try it out. Still, she remained cautious. "How would it work?"

"Well, I think we both know how it would work. We just have to try it. Carefully, of course. I don't want you to be scared." He smiled. "After all, a nervous cow is a poor producer."

She laughed at his little joke and felt the trust grow between them. "Yes. I agree. But I guess I'm a bit curious to see this equipment you developed."

"Come with me," he said, and led her by the hand outside. She couldn't remember the last time a man had held her hand. Dusk was gathering around them. His farm spread out before her, surrounded by trees and illuminated by a half-moon. It was all quite romantic, although Brenda tried not to notice. This was a business arrangement, wasn't it?

He took her to the barn and showed her how he had set it up.

"Look. I've build individual stalls, with straw and some comfortable blankets. This is heated in the winter for maximum comfort."

It was just as she had envisioned it in her wildest imaginings. She could picture herself lying in the hay, wrapped in a blanket, waiting for her next milking.

But wait. Wasn't it all too much? It was one thing to dream about it, but quite another to actually do it. She might simply feel foolish, not aroused. Some dreams should not come true. Maybe she should just go home and get her old job back at the hospital.

Then Brenda's eyes focused on the strange apparatus set up in the center of the room. It consisted of a small wooden frame set over a long rubber mat. Inside the frame, lying loose on the ground were two half-spheres connected by hoses to a machine near a workbench. Jack caught her gaze.

"Oh, I see you've spotted my invention. A human milking machine." Brenda felt a throb of heat in her loins. "Let me show how it works." He described how the woman crouches on her hands and knees on the rubber pad while the specially designed milking devices attach to each breast.

My god, Brenda thought—it's just like my dream!

"I can assure you, these took years to develop," he told her. He was preaching to the choir. Her hands were already fingering the cups, her mind racing, her thighs clamped tightly together.

"Would you like to see how they work?" he asked and her knee-jerk reaction was to refuse out of embarrassment.

"Uh, I don't know. It's a bit sudden."

Then she saw his gentle expression and realized he was just trying to help her live out her childhood fantasy. And probably his, as well.

He shrugged. "Or not. If you feel uncomfortable..."

"No." The word burst out of her. Did she dare reveal her darkest secret to this man? "I'm just shy. That's all."

Jack put a hand on her upper arm. "Hey now. It's me, remember? I'm your friend. We've talked around this subject for months without coming right out and admitting it. But I know."

She looked into his eyes and realized it was true.

"I know that the idea of being milked is highly arousing to you. You can't explain it. It just is. Well, the idea turns me on too. And I can't explain it either." He laughed. "Why do you think I turned my farm over to a bunch of lactating women? I don't get to watch, but I get a thrill just knowing they're in the next room, being milked. And I've spent far too much time developing these," he said, pointing to the cups. "If anyone should be called perverted, it's me."

Her heart opened up then. They were soulmates! Her hands went to her blouse and began fumbling with the buttons.

"Here, allow me."

She didn't stop him when he began to unbutton her blouse. It came off her shoulders like a woman who wanted to be stripped. The large bra held her breasts tight against her chest. "Here now, that looks uncomfortable. May I?"

He had asked so politely, she could only nod, the blood roaring in her ears. He was right, her bra did hurt. When he reached around back and unfastened it, she almost wept with relief when it came loose, freeing her breasts. She knew, for the first time, that this man would not cringe at the sight of her large mounds. He would know how to handle them. Brenda stood erect in front of him, fighting the voice inside that told her she was too fat and listened to the one that told her she would be an excellent producer of milk for the little babies.

"Magnificent," Jack breathed. His hands came up and began to stroke her. She closed her eyes and felt the heat build up in her loins. Her body shook with desire. She could happily fuck this man right now. She told herself that he probably wasn't interested in her that way. Having him touch her breasts was enough, she thought.

He continued to massage her, using his fingers to gently pull on the nipples. Brenda felt her bones melt and her knees grow weak. She wanted to sit down.

He noticed. "Here," he said. "Let's try it for a minute, shall we? You won't produce any milk, of course, until we begin treatments, but you can get a sense of what it's like."

She nodded dreamily, willing to do almost anything for this man. He eased her down onto the rubber pad on her hands and knees, her breasts hanging down. He squatted down next to her so he could continue to stroke her, driving her wild. Then she felt him pull away for a moment and opened her eyes to see him smear some waxy material onto his hands. When his fingers returned to spread it over her breasts and nipples, Brenda felt on the verge of an orgasm. *Would he think less of me if I came right now?* She struggled to hold off.

He seemed to read her mind. "It's okay. Let go. Don't fight it on my account."

She almost came right then—only her shyness prevented her from climaxing in front of this man she had only met in person that day. His touch, she knew, would soon overcome her reticence. But he pulled away at the last minute, causing her to make a soft sound in her throat. Jack brought the cups up into position. In the background, she heard the sound of a motor. "Here, these attach by suction. I've been told they feel pretty good."

She didn't protest as he fitted them over her breasts. The interiors were soft and gently sucked at her flesh until a seal was formed. Her nipples were vacuumed down into the base of the cups, but she felt only pleasure as they stretched slightly. She recalled the cows at the dairy farm, waiting patiently for the machines and understood now why they didn't complain.

"That's just the suction part. Now comes the actual milking, if you had milk, of course." He flipped another switch and her nipples seemed to come alive.

"Oh, god," she breathed, feeling the nipples being tugged alternately. "Ohhh, that's so nice." She began to breathe rapidly, her body shaking with desire. She was on the edge, ready to fall over the cliff. Suddenly, she felt his hand pressing tightly against the crotch of her jeans and that was all it took. She gasped and came, hard, her body shaking as she cried out. "Oh god, oh god, oh god!" Her arms would no longer support her and she collapsed to her elbows, her face down on the mat.

He leaned down to whisper. "Think how much better that would feel if you were actually producing milk. And if you were kept naked, so I could help you come whenever you were on the machine."

Brenda looked up at him in disbelief. Her fantasy could come true, if she would only allow it. "Please," she gasped at last. "When can we start?"

CHAPTER THREE

Brenda moved in immediately. Jack gave her a stall and took her suitcase, chiding her, "Cows don't wear clothes. I'll store this up at the house for you."

He stood over her and she felt suddenly small. "Now, about the rest of your clothes,' he said, his voice light. She giggled and handed them over, suddenly no longer embarrassed about her body. Jack was only the second man ever to see her completely naked and she marveled at how relaxed she felt. Of course, having such a powerful orgasm at his hands helped.

He went to a small refrigerator that had a lock set into it. Taking a key from his pocket, he unlocked it and took out a vial. Finding a syringe from a drawer, he approached her. "Hey, you're probably a better expert at this than me. In order to stimulate milk production, I need to inject you with ten cc's of this every day."

She looked at the label and nodded. She recognized the name of a common USDA-approved drug to improve lactation—one she had been tempted to take many times while working at the hospital, but hadn't for fear her secret might get out. As a nurse's aide, she also knew it was unwise to self-medicate without outside supervision.

She unwrapped the needle and expertly sucked the right amount into the syringe. Tapping it and squirting out a fine stream, she turned and aimed it at her generous hip and plunged the needle home. She barely winced as she pressed the solution into her.

"There," she said, handing him the empty syringe and vial. "I can feel it working already." She giggled.

He laughed with her. Tossing the needle in the biohazard container, he replaced the vial in the fridge and closed it. "Okay. That's it. Now, I'm sure you're hungry, so I'll bring you some food.

We need to keep your strength up." Then he snapped his fingers. "Oh, I almost forgot." He returned to the fridge and retrieved a quart bottle of water. "This has some electrolytes in it to help you produce milk. You'll need to drink a lot of fluids, you know."

Brenda nodded. She had said the same thing many times to the new mothers she had counseled.

"Well, I'd better leave you alone for the night, let that stuff work." He closed the stall door. Brenda noted that it wasn't locked—she could leave at any time.

She looked around the stall and said cautiously. "Um, what about, you know, going to the bathroom?"

"Cows pee and poop right in their stall. Don't worry, I'll clean it out regularly. This is part of the whole experience, right? You really owe it to yourself to try it out. That's all we're doing."

She laughed at the thought of her acting the part of a dairy cow. Was it really happening? "I guess so. I'm glad it's summer. I might freeze to death out here otherwise."

"Don't worry. The barn is heated. If it gets chilly, it comes on automatically."

He left and returned a few minutes later with several pieces of chicken in the bottom of a KFC bucket. He handed it over the stall and she took it gratefully. "Eat all you want. The more protein you have, the more milk you can produce." She nodded and dove into the chicken. "See you in the morning." Jack left and turned out the lights, all except for a small one above her stall and another one near the door.

She sat on her haunches, naked, sweating slightly in the heat as she ate. If she had a mirror, she might've been shocked at her image. When she finished, she settled down into her blanket. Brenda pulled it around her and wondered if she was going too far with all this. It did feel sexy and naughty, she told herself.

You worry too much.

The next morning, she debated going outside to pee, rather than mess up her stall. It just seemed wrong somehow. She left the stall and went to the door and peeked out. Her nerve failed her. Somehow, being naked in a barn, pretending to be a cow was one thing, but going outside naked and squatting to relieve herself in full view of god knows who was something else. She returned to her stall and peed in a corner.

Brenda waited patiently for Jack to return. Her breasts felt a little tight and she imagined the solution was working. She hoped it wouldn't take long. Looking through the slats of her stall, she could picture herself hooked up to the machine again, this time watching as thin white milk flowed out into the tubes. God, the idea made her hot! One hand went to her breasts and began stroking. Her other hand reached between her legs and touched her wetness. Her mind drifted. Rubbing quickly, she brought herself to an orgasm, panting in the early morning heat.

Jack came out about ten minutes later. His expression was stern, which surprised Brenda. "What's wrong?"

"I watched you on the monitor," he said, pointing up to a corner of her stall. She glanced up and was shocked to see a small camera mounted there. She hadn't noticed it before.

"You're watching me? Why?"

"I want to help you with this experience. Consider it part of the training for a new milk cow." He smiled.

Brenda was confused. This was just a game, after all—wasn't it? "Training?"

"You did two things wrong. I'm not sure you're going to make a good cow."

"What do you mean?"

"One, you left the stall. Cows can't do that. Two, you masturbated. I saw you." He smiled slyly and waggled his finger at her. "Cows don't masturbate. They wait to be masturbated. Like yesterday."

She felt a rush of relief. He wanted to make her come himself! "Oh, yes, sir," she said with mock seriousness. "By all means." Her loins tingled with the thought that his fingers would soon be touching her naked sex again.

"Good girl. But now you're all done. There's no point in hooking you up to the machine."

"Ohh, no, please, Jack. I didn't know. Don't worry, I can come again. That was just a warm-up. I was thinking about being naked in the machine, and having you touch me."

"If you're going to be my cow, you're going to have to learn the rules. I can't very well reward you now." His words seemed at odds with his teasing tone.

"Please?"

He thought for a moment. "Tell you what. In order to counteract you leaving the stall on your own and the self-pleasuring, you'd have to agree to a bit of punishment before I could in good conscience put you on the machine. Don't you think?"

That stopped her. "W-what kind of punishment?"

Jack walked to the worktable and returned with a riding crop, about eighteen inches long. "How about ten swats with this?"

Brenda eyed him cautiously. Did he really want to do that? Was this part of her fantasy—or his? Perhaps she should call a halt to this. Then she thought about the drugs working to turn her into a milk producer and didn't want to give that up yet. She had come so far to get to this point.

"You want to hit me with that?"

"Yes. You'll find, I think, that it can be highly arousing."

Brenda considered that. She had seen such things on the Internet and she knew a lot of women got off on it. Men too. "You won't hit me too hard, will you?"

"No, I just want to make you realize that you can only come at my command. I can't have my cows getting themselves off whenever they feel like it."

She smiled tentatively. Well, she told herself, she was living her fantasy, is it so wrong to allow Jack to live his? "Okay. But go easy."

Jack opened up her stall door and motioned to her. She came out slowly, feeling a tinge of fear for the first time since she had arrived.

"Go kneel on the mat, face down, ass up."

Brenda went and did as he bid, her body shaking slightly.

"Legs farther apart." She hustled to obey.

"I'm going to give you five for leaving the stall and five for masturbating. You are not to move or I'll have to start over. You understand?"

"Yes," she squeaked.

Whap! The first swat wasn't hard, but it startled her. She jerked and cried out.

"That wasn't very hard. I can do it much harder."

"I know. I was just startled."

Whap! She managed to stay still this time. "That was one, since you jerked on the first one."

She vowed not to give him any further reason to add to her punishment. She took the next nine swats without moving or crying out, though it hurt terribly after the fifth stroke. If anything, Jack seemed to increase the power of his blows.

"Okay, you're done. Now you can get into the machine."

Brenda scooted into position, her ass aflame. It wasn't as bad as she had imagined. Combined with the tingle in her breasts, she felt almost euphoric. She couldn't explain it. She should be appalled or angry. Instead, she felt more like an animal. She realized Jack was using operant conditioning on her, to make her more obedient. Like a cow should be. She waited on her hands and knees, her body trembling with the thought. This won't just be a game that she controls, she realized. Jack was taking charge. She wasn't sure how she felt about it. On one hand, she wanted to control the pace of this experiment. On the other hand, having a strong man such as Jack direct her made her feel small and delicate. That only increased her desire.

He gave her the hormone shot, then came forward and began to massage her breasts, rubbing in that wonderful salve. Coming right on the heels of being "punished," she felt sexier now, more pliable. She wanted to please him, so she knelt there motionless while he stroked her.

Her nipples extended! under his gentle touch. He tugged on them, as if he could make them longer by doing so. Brenda could feel that familiar heat in her pussy and hoped he would make her come again.

"Now, you know that your breasts aren't ready yet. We'll probably have to give you shots for a week or two before milk will flow. But by putting you in the machine twice a day, even just for a few minutes, it will help stimulate your breasts."

"Okay," she breathed. She didn't care, just do it, she thought. Brenda's body throbbed now, waiting for the cups to be attached. Finally, Jack got up to retrieve them. Her breasts seemed to cry out in relief. He flipped the switch and the low hum of the motor only increased her orgasmic state. She was becoming like one of Pavlov's dogs, salivating at the mere sound of the suction machine. Or, in her case, rising up toward an orgasm.

When he fitted the cup over her left breast, Brenda groaned aloud.

"Now don't come yet. I wouldn't want to have to spank you again."

That chilled her. Her thoughts became jumbled. Her orgasm retreated, only to return when he fitted the second cup on her right breast. Her nipples were pulled down inside and Brenda's mouth came open. Was it the spanking, combined with the suction that was arousing her so?

"Oh, god, Jack, I think I'm going to come."

"Not yet!" He gave her a slap on her sore ass, delaying her pleasure. "See if you can stand it for three minutes this time."

She nodded, but she really didn't think she could do it. She wanted him to touch her between her legs. She would explode if he did. When he flipped on the switch, activating the nipple stimulators, Brenda groaned again, gritting her teeth to keep from coming. "Oh my god, Jack!"

He slapped her ass again, and again. Each time, she felt caught in the middle, trying not to give into the pleasure she so desperately needed. Each minute seemed to crawl by and she was visibly shaking, hanging on by her fingertips.

Then, when she was sure she could stand it no longer, Jack stopped slapping her ass and brought his fingers hard up against her wet clit, saying at the same time, "Come for me, cow, come for me."

"OH MY GOD!" The orgasm ripped through her like a freight train, rendering her nearly unconscious. Her arms gave way and her head and shoulders flopped to the mat, her mind shattered by the power of her climax. For several minutes, she knelt there, unaware of the soft sucking sound of the machine, feeling only her nipples gently being kneaded. She was limp, used up.

She didn't notice when Jack got up to turn off the machine and eased the cups from her throbbing breasts.

"Good girl. You're going to make a great cow. I'm very proud of you."

He left her there for a while so she could recover on her own. When he returned, she was still on the mat, snoring softly. He poked her with one foot. She came awake and looked up, blearily. "Oh, hi. Wow. What hit me?"

"That is what happens when you combine a woman's secret desire with her underutilized sex drive," he said, smiling down at her.

She laughed. "Boy, I've never come like that before, even with a vibrator."

"Stick with me and you'll have those all the time."

"I'm not sure I could stand it." But she thought she could.

CHAPTER FOUR

The week passed slowly. Brenda got used to the hay, the dust, the daily shots, the "training" with the riding crop—all happily endured in exchange for one powerful orgasm after another at Jack's hands. She rarely had to be punished twice for some transgression, but Jack always seemed to come up with new rules for her. For example, he told her cows don't walk upright, forcing her to crawl around the barn on her hands and knees or endure the crop. She humored him at first, but whenever her knees grew sore and she tried to stand, he would be on her, striking her until she sunk back down.

Later, when he told her to go outside and she balked at the door, suddenly ashamed of her nudity, Jack immediately spanked her with the crop until she practically ran outside, scraping her knees painfully on the doorsill. He ordered her into a small grassy pasture and began to hose her down. She sputtered and protested, but he told her it was either this or stay dirty.

It surprised her that she didn't protest more. By all rights, she should have put an end to the game and gone home. But the fulfillment of her long-denied fantasy hadn't lost its power yet. Besides, no one had ever made her come like that before and she knew, deep down, that no one else ever would. She was an ugly duckling, a human castoff. She considered herself lucky to have found Jack, a man who genuinely seemed to like her. Her only regret so far was that he hadn't fucked her yet. Every time she was on the machine, rising toward another bone-shaking orgasm, she hoped he would take her quickly from behind, but he used his hand only for the first few days. Still, the orgasms were wonderful.

The change came on the fifth day. By now, she was already conditioned to obey him without question. When it came time for her morning "milking"—with no milk evident yet—she crawled out happily from her stall and got into position on the mat. He had been extending the time she was dry-milked, until she was up to about seven minutes per session. Jack gave her a tall glass of water, mixed with electrolytes, as usual, then attached the cups and started the machine, but this time, he used leather straps to tie her arms and legs to the wooden frame, trapping her into position. Brenda started to protest, but Jack just shook his head and she decided it wasn't worth arguing about. After all, where would she go? She didn't want to move anyway, once those wonderful cups were attached.

Then he surprised her. He took off his pants and moved behind her. She turned to look at him, seeing his rock-hard cock. He swatted her with the riding crop he always seemed to carry. "Don't look back. Concentrate on your udders. Don't come yet."

She nodded and let the sensations wash through her. But when she felt the tip of his cock touch her sopping wet opening, she began to shudder, desperately trying to hold back her climax. He struck her on her rump, breaking the mood for a second. Then his cock returned and she hovered there, on the edge, hanging on by her fingertips. Now she knew why she had been tied in place—she might have tried to pull away on order to prevent her orgasm—or plunge back to satisfy her lust. He had wanted her to be completely helpless.

"God, Jack, my god."

Whap!

Another thirty seconds passed. "Oh, no, I'm going to come, I can't—"

WHAP! WHAP!

Her nipples seemed to have a direct connection to her desperate cunt. With Jack poised there, the tip just touching her, her pussy seemed to reach out for him. "Please," she begged.

WHAP!

He was determined to control her. So she let him. In her mind, she just let go of herself and waited for his command. Her climax poised there like a beast, waiting for the word to be unleashed. But it was only his word that could free it.

She knew she had been on the machine for several minutes now and guessed she was about done. Her nipples had just begun to ache when Jack suddenly thrust into her all at once and cried out, "Come, cow, come for me!"

The shock of his cock sliding into her, combined with the massaging of her nipples, and the sound of his voice giving her permission caused a huge explosion within her. She bellowed as the climax rocked her, yanking at her bonds and shuddering with pleasure. The orgasm seemed to bounce around inside her until she was senseless with it. Part of her mind shouted: *He's fucking me! He's fucking me!*

"OH GOD! OH GOD! OH GOD!" she cried, over and over again. Sweat poured off her body. She sagged in her straps, unable to hold herself up. She drifted in and out of consciousness for a few seconds. Inside her, she could feel Jack pumping away. She came alert as a second orgasm approached. She pushed back as best she could and waited. Jack's thrusts increased and Brenda thought the top of her head would fly off.

He grabbed her hips and plunged deep into her. She could feel his cock erupt, his seed filling her womb. She came again and cried out, calling his name over and over. Sweat pooled around her hands and knees as it sluiced off of her.

When she was more coherent, at long last, she gasped, "Oh, Jack, that was wonderful!"

He pulled out and moved away. She could feel his semen start to drip from her pussy and smiled at the sensation. She had been fucked at long last! He returned with a cup and held it between her legs, collecting it. Brenda thought that was very odd, but didn't say anything. She waited to be untied.

More of the semen dripped into the cup. Jack patiently collected it. When he had captured all he could, he showed her the contents, tipping it down in front of her eyes. "See, not too bad. A tablespoon or so."

"Uh huh," she said, nonplussed.

"Here, suck me off." He came forward and she eagerly took him into her mouth, enjoying the taste of him. She didn't mind her own taste on him.

Jack went to the refrigerator and pulled out a chocolate protein drink. She watched as he poured it into a tall glass. This was nothing new—he routinely gave her one after each milking session. He told her it would help her milk production, but Brenda thought she was just getting fatter. Certainly her breasts were getting bigger!

Then Jack did something that shocked her. He took the cup and poured the goopy semen mixture into it! She gasped out loud. "I'm not drinking that!" she said at once.

Jack put the drink down on the workbench and picked up the riding crop. Brenda's heart fell. "What did you say?" he asked with a hint of warning.

"Uh. Okay, I'll drink it. But could you stir it up, please?"

"Of course. He stuck his finger in it and twirled it around. She grimaced but said nothing. He approached and held the glass for her. It was awkward, but she managed to drink it down while still tied into position. It didn't taste bad at all. She could barely tell there was semen in it.

"Good girl," he said when she was finished. He untied her and led her outside to her small section of pasture next to the barn. This time of day the sun beat down on it. Brenda was worried about sunburn, but Jack was always a step ahead of her. He tossed her a tube of sunscreen. "Just until your skin gets used to the sun," he told her.

That afternoon and the next morning, during her regular dry milkings, Jack again fucked her while she was strapped to the machine. Her orgasms were as intense as the first time and she realized that she had had more sex in the last few days here than she had had in her entire life before. Afterwards, she gently sucked his cock clean, as it had become part of their routine.

Although some of the humiliations, rules and punishments were a bit much, Brenda felt satisfaction on a deep level that had previously been only a fantasy. She was more than willing to give Jack control over her, as long as he fucked her so readily. Perhaps he would make her pregnant and they would live happily ever after. She wasn't taking any birth control, she knew that. Let whatever happens happen, she thought.

It was during her afternoon milking a few days later that events began to diverge from her fantasies. She was strapped in, as usual, cups attached, machine humming away, while she waited for Jack to move behind her and tease her with his cock. Instead, he stayed next to her and stroked her back. It was soothing and she enjoyed the attention, but she really wanted to be fucked and fucked hard. Still, she knew better than to question him.

Brenda was falling into a stupor, feeling the nipples being worked and Jack's hand on her back and shoulders, when she heard a noise behind her. She started to turn, but Jack stopped her, saying, "Shhhh, just relax."

When she felt something touch her naked wet slit, she jerked in her bonds and asked, "What's going on?" Then she felt hands on her and she turned, despite Jack's order. She was shocked to see another man, a stranger, kneeling behind her, naked from the waist down, his hard cock jutting out. And it was quite big! She'd never seen anything like it before, although, admittedly, her experience was limited.

"What the—" She glared at Jack. "Jack!"

"Shhh," he repeated. "This is Charlie. He's helping me out, because, as you can see, he has a very large cock. A big woman like you needs someone who can satisfy her better."

"Nooo!" She struggled to get away, but the straps held her firm. Tears sprang from her eyes.

"It's all right. He's only going to tease you, to help you produce milk. He won't fuck you unless you tell him too, okay?"

She nodded, happy to have at least some control. "Okay."

"Now, concentrate on your tits. Feel the nipples being worked. You could start letting down any day now. This will help."

So she did. She tried to ignore Charlie's presence behind her. He had moved away during her protest, but now she could feel his cock return to bump against her well-lubricated opening. God, his cock did feel large, she noted, larger than Jack's. She wondered how it might feel, up inside her. The thought shocked her, even as it flashed across her mind.

Jack continued to stroke her back and between his touch, the gentle kneading of her breasts and the teasing of Charlie's cock, Brenda felt another orgasm building. She went with it, riding along on that magic carpet toward climax, which her body had come to demand. How could she have lived so many years without them, except the ones she had given herself?

Charlie's cock was moving up and down against her slit, smearing the wetness there and driving her crazy. Maybe she should let him, she thought. What could it hurt? Jack certainly didn't mind. He was practically encouraging her!

"Oh god, oh god..." she whispered, feeling the waves of pleasure building within her. She wasn't sure which felt better, Charlie's cock or her tits.

Then a new noise invaded her reverie—a sucking sound.

"Congratulations, my cow, you are now producing milk," Jack said.

She glanced down at the tubes leading away from the cups on her breasts and saw a few traces of thin white fluid being produced. "God! Oh, god!" she breathed, feeling the orgasm begin to rush at her now, building up like a tsunami to engulf her.

Jack leaned close and whispered, "Go ahead, tell Charlie you want him to fuck you, you know you want to."

The man's cock was insistent, rubbing her, teasing her, torturing her. Jack was right—she wanted it inside her. Brenda gasped, her mind slipping away. "Fu-fu-fu-," she managed.

"What was that? Remember, you have to ask."

"Fuck, fuck, fuck…" Still the cock rubbed the outside of her sopping wet cunt. She rotated her hips to encourage him, but he wouldn't take the hint. "God. Oh god." She thought she might pass out.

"Come on, cow, let yourself go."

"Fuck me! FUCK ME!" she shouted, and felt Charlie's hard cock thrust into her, all the way to the hilt. Her eyes popped open. It *was* huge! It filled her so completely, like nothing she'd ever felt before. Instantly, the orgasm exploded within her, causing her to shake in her bonds and nearly pass out. He kept pumping and another climax struck her, then a third. Sweat poured off of her and she pressed back to meet his thrusts. His calloused hands gripped her ass tightly, rocking her in the frame, the straps pulling at her upper arms and thighs.

Then Jack must've loosened them, for she felt her legs come free, followed by her arms and she really began to thrust herself on his cock, jerking back and forth as his hands steered his meat into her. Another orgasm struck, and another.

"Ah, ah, ah, ah…" she vocalized, her mind reduced to its lowest level—a brain stem with tits and a cunt attached.

Charlie suddenly plunged into her hard, his hands like talons on her ass, and she could feel his sperm splashing into her womb, again and again. Despite her exhaustion, she came again with him, and collapsed onto the frame, her ass still held in his grip, his cock deep within her.

"God! She's good," Charlie said. It was the first words he spoken since he had arrived. He slipped his softening cock out and brought it around to her front. She knew what he wanted. Brenda pushed herself upright and took his wet member into her mouth and licked him dry. Even flaccid, his cock was impressive. But she didn't understand why Jack would do that—his cock had been fine. Or at least, she hadn't known the difference until now. It puzzled her that Jack would volunteer to bring in a man that made him inadequate by comparison.

Jack was behind her now, holding the cup up to collect the fluids that dripped from her. She grimaced, for she knew what that meant. She was embarrassed to be asked to drink it in front of Charlie.

He held the cup up for her to see. "Looks like a bit more than I've been producing. Charlie's a real firehose, isn't he?"

Brenda nodded vacantly, her face red. She glanced past him to see Charlie nonchalantly zipping up his pants.

Jack went to the refrigerator and pulled out a protein drink. Vanilla, this time. But he surprised her when he only poured half of it into the glass before adding the semen mixture.

"What—"

He shushed her and held the cup for her. Since she was untied now, she reached out for it. He pulled it back and shook his head. So she allowed him to hold it to her lips and she drank it down. Brenda had forgotten to ask him to stir it up, so the semen lay like cream on the top, adding a slightly bitter taste. When she was finished, he added the rest of the can and made her drink that down. She didn't understand Jack's logic, but said nothing.

The bell dinged, indicating her session with the pump was over. Jack unhooked her and besides the ache in her nipples, her breasts felt empty for the first time. He showed her small vial where the milk had been collected. "Just a couple of tablespoons or so. But it's a good start. Soon you'll be producing milk for many babies."

Brenda beamed with pride and her sex with a total stranger was forgotten for a moment. Charlie left without another word and Jack led Brenda out to the pasture for the last few hours of sun left. She wanted to ask him if he would ever fuck her again, or just let Charlie do it, but the words died on her tongue.

She was learning.

CHAPTER FIVE

Brenda's fears proved true. Charlie became her only lover for the next several sessions. Although "lover" was hardly the word for it. He just fucked her and left. She still didn't know anything about him. He barely spoke. But she had become intimately acquainted with his cock and the taste of his seed. And, of course, his hands as they gripped her ass.

She no longer turned around now when she felt him approach. He always came in from behind and suddenly, his hands would be on her, his cock thrusting into her. Jack stopped tying her to the frame, so she could thrust back against him and achieve her much-needed orgasms. For now, he just watched and never joined in. She missed his cock and wished he would fuck her as well.

Her breasts had swelled until they looked out of place on her chest. They were producing more milk now and it seemed to increase with every session. He kept her well fed and watered and Brenda knew she was gaining weight. But she didn't care. If she got pregnant—now it would be Charlie's baby, she realized—she would need the extra protein.

He still washed her off outside, although she noticed that it occurred with less frequency. Sometimes three days would go by before he cleaned her and he never allowed her soap. She began to get used to being dirty much of the time. Charlie didn't seem to care. The only part of her that was regularly cleaned were her breasts, for the cups needed clean skin to attach to.

Brenda had become so complacent about being fucked while Jack watched that she didn't raise a protest when he brought out a video camera and began filming as Charlie entered her. Afterwards, he rewound the film and showed it to her on the small screen. She was embarrassed, seeing herself smeared with dirt, acting like a slut and an animal, rutting with this near-stranger while her tits gurgled out their milk. Then again, she realized, she was an animal. That's why she was here, to fulfill her fantasy.

Except the fantasy seemed to be taking on a life of its own.

It was about a week later, during an afternoon session, that he led her into the frame and began to buckle the straps.

She turned to him at once, "You don't need to do that."

He took the riding crop and spanked her several times on her rump, saying only, "Shhhh." So she quieted down and let him strap her in. Her stomach flip-flopped, for she knew something was coming.

But when the pump was activated and her milk began to flow, Brenda went into her stupor and pushed her doubts out of her mind. She waited for Charlie and his wonderful cock. She could almost feel it inside her again. A few seconds later, she was not disappointed when she felt the tip of a cock rub against her. She pressed back, as best she could, and the cock slipped in.

Her eyes widened. This wasn't Charlie's cock! It was somewhat smaller, she could tell right away. And the rhythm of his coupling was different. She started to turn around, but Jack rapped her thigh sharply in warning. So she stared straight ahead and let the man fuck her. She felt used and humiliated, but she couldn't deny the orgasm that tickled her. Could she bring it forward? She concentrated on her breasts and her cunt and found it growing within her.

Suddenly, the man erupted within her, long before she was ready. He pulled out and she sagged in her bonds, thinking she wouldn't be allowed to climax today. Her mouth opened in shock when she felt another pair of hands on her ass, another cock enter her. Again, she tried to turn and again Jack struck her with the crop. As if to punish her further, he took out a bandana and tied it over her eyes, blinding her.

God! He was turning her into a slut! To what purpose? All she had wanted was Jack, or maybe Charlie. Now two other men—strangers—were taking her. She wondered how many were back there, in line, when she felt something bump against her face. She knew at once—it was the first man's soft cock, waiting for her to clean it off. Brenda wanted to refuse, only to feel Jack rub the riding crop over her back in warning. Sighing, she opened her mouth and took him in.

When the second man finished, a third one stepped up. Then a fourth. And a fifth. Brenda was frustrated and angry now. She had been unable to climax, even if she had wanted to. So she saw herself simply as a receptacle for their sperm. She was given no time between men—as soon as one finished, another one moved up. Then she'd be forced to clean them off and not all of them seemed to bathe regularly. Tied in as she was, she couldn't shake them off, so she had to endure the torment.

When the sixth man rubbed up against her, she thought the recognized the cock. Could it be? Yes! It was Charlie. At least he felt familiar! Brenda thought she might be able to climax at last. She began to rock with him, meeting his thrusts. Jack came forward to untie her and she smiled gratefully. Now they moved together as one, her orgasm came roaring back. It didn't take long before she came once, then twice at his cock. When he erupted within her, she felt completely drained.

But no. Her ordeal was not over yet. When Charlie stepped away, Jack was between her legs again, collecting the copious fluids that jetted from her sore and wide-open cunt. Surely he wouldn't make her drink that! Even mixed with her drink, it would be vile.

"Jack…" She began and was rewarded with several sharp slaps with the crop to her ass. In the background, she heard several men laugh. They were all still there, watching her! She cringed and tried to make herself smaller.

"Get up on your knees," he ordered and she knew he was holding her drink for her. She rose up, her face showing her distaste, even behind her blindfold. She felt the cup at her lips. "Drink this. If you spill any, you will be punished."

Why was he being so mean! This isn't what she had signed up for! "No," she said at once, pushing him away. "I want to go home. I've had enough."

Suddenly, two men on either side of her grabbed her arms and held her tight. A third pulled her head back and pinched her nose, forcing her mouth to open as she gulped air. She tried to fight them, but they were too strong. She felt the contents of the cup being poured down her throat. Very little protein drink had been mixed in this time, she could tell at once. It was almost all semen, from six different men, and there was a great deal of it. She sputtered and coughed, but most of it went down. The men let her go and she sagged down.

This wasn't fun any longer. "I want to go home," she repeated. "I'm all done."

She heard the shuffling of feet and realized the men were leaving. When it grew quiet, Jack untied her blindfold and pulled it free. Brenda looked around. The barn was empty except for the two of them. She turned her gaze to Jack. "You went too far," she said. "This wasn't part of the deal."

"I believe it is," he said. "And I'll tell you why. Yes, I am pushing you, and I'm pretty sure a secret part of you likes it, but is ashamed to admit it. Remember, you came to me. I told you what kind of place I had here and what I really wanted from you. You said you wanted to try it out."

"Being milked! Pretending to be a cow—that's what I wanted to try! Not fucking strangers."

"It's all part of my plan to give you what you secretly need. Let me ask you this: Have you ever had such intense orgasms in your life before?"

Even in her anger, Brenda had to admit to herself she hadn't. She didn't say anything, but Jack could read it on her face.

"And the milkings, and living in a barn—those things all satisfy your inner urges, don't they?"

She nodded. "But not all the men," she finally said. "It makes me feel a slut."

"Like I said, I know what I'm doing. I have my reasons and they will be made clear to you at the right time." He shrugged. "But if you want to call it quits, I can put you on a bus back home tomorrow."

It surprised her that it would be so easy. Just quit. Go back to her old life and start over. *Sure, that's what I'll do,* she thought *Leave this crazy episode behind me. I may be a lot of things, but a cheap slut I am not!*

Then another voice in her head spoke up: *Go back to what? Working for near-minimum wage every day and being lonely every night? Look forward to a life where the only sexual stimulation is from your own hand?*

Her breasts began to ache, as if they were telling her they wanted to stay as well. Now that they had finally let down some milk, she wanted to call it off? She opened her mouth to speak, but no sound came out.

Jack reached out and touched her shoulder. "I know you are confused. I know it's been hard. I'm not a kidnapper, so you are free to leave, if you really want to. But I think I know you pretty well by now. I know you'd get back there and be lonely and disappointed. You'd miss this life, the sex, the breast stimulations. You need what I offer, Brenda."

"But it's so hard. I'm not like that. I don't sleep around. I could get pregnant, you know."

"No, actually, you can't. I've taken the liberty of putting birth control pills in the water you've been drinking every day. And none of the men have any diseases, I've had them all tested. I wouldn't want to harm my prize milk producer."

Surprisingly, instead of being angry for his underhanded actions, Brenda was secretly pleased. It took away some the worries she had. Her mind bounced back and forth, trying to decide what to do.

Jack stepped back. "If you decide to stay, it will be under my conditions. Otherwise, you're free to go." He paused. "Would you like to take some time to think about it?"

"Yeah," she said absently, rubbing her large, empty breasts. "If I go, what will happen to my milk—I mean, my breasts?" She already knew the answer, she just wanted to hear Jack confirm it.

"Oh, I imagine they will ache for a while, and probably continue to produce milk, until the hormones wear off. You'll probably have to milk them yourself for a time. But they'll eventually return to normal."

Brenda thought about that. She had finally achieved her dream to produce milk and now she was going to give it up? She hardly noticed when Jack led her out to the pasture, her mind racing. She slumped down on the grass in the shade and tried to think. Her breasts felt sated and her cunt throbbed. She needed time to sort things out. Absently, her hand drifted down to touch her clit, which pulsed contentedly with the pleasure she had been given.

And why not? that other voice inside her broke in. *Now that you know Jack is watching out for you, why not let yourself go? Do you think you're going to get this kind of attention anywhere else?*

When it came time to go in for the evening, she still hadn't made up her mind. Jack didn't question her, he merely led her inside to her stall and shut the gate behind her. She curled up on the blanket and tried to sleep.

The next morning, her breasts ached from being full. They seemed to have swelled in the night. God, the thought of leaving and not being able to have her breasts milked sent a dagger to her heart. Maybe she could stay a little while longer, she mused, just until my milk production grows. Let me contribute to the babies' needs. Later, she could taper off.

While she thought about a delay in leaving, she squatted in the corner of her stall and relieved herself. It seemed almost normal now to empty her bladder and bowels on the straw. Jack was very good about replacing it regularly, keeping the odors down.

When he came in, she stood up to greet him, in defiance of the rules. "I've been thinking," she said as he opened the stall door. "I'm considering staying for a little longer, just until my milk really starts to flow. Maybe a couple more weeks. Then I'll go."

"No," he said simply.

"W-what do you mean, no?" She was indignant.

"This is a one-time offer. I can't have you vacillating. Either you want to stay and experience what I can offer you or you leave now, never to return."

Never to return? Always, in the back of her mind, Brenda had imagined that if she had gone home and realized her mistake, that Jack would welcome her back with open arms. "So you're saying that either I agree to be your cow forever or I'm banished forever?"

"I didn't say you'd be my cow forever. Only as long as you were productive and you were getting what you need from this experience. But as for the other side of that, yes. If you leave here today, you can't come back."

"But, but..." She tailed off. "Why?"

"Because right now you are at a critical stage. You are still Brenda, the nurse's aide from Alabama. You still think of yourself as human, playing at being a milk producer. If you stay, you're going to have to give up all that and become a real cow, whose main duty is to produce milk for undernourished infants."

He paused and gave her a level gaze. "I think you want to, but you are afraid of stepping off that cliff. I'm here to give you that push—or to haul you away from the edge and send you home. It's your decision." He jerked his head to indicate she should come out. "In the meantime, let's say we milk you, okay?"

She nodded and followed him to the machine, glancing over her shoulder toward the back doors, wondering if those men would be returning. Jack laughed. "Don't worry, it's just you and me today. I thought you could use the break."

He got an electrolyte drink from the fridge and watched as she drank it down. Then he moved up to wash her heavy breasts in preparation for her milking. She closed her eyes, her thoughts confused. She wanted to feed the babies, but she worried about giving up her sense of self.

"If I stay," she said softly, "what more might you require of me?"

"Total obedience," he said at once. "You want to live like a cow, I will allow it—but on my terms. Not yours. You would have to agree to my training. Like I said, I have a plan."

Brenda wasn't sure she could do that. It was a lot to ask. But she didn't want to go home either. She was torn. Jack began stroking her breasts, spreading the salve on them. She closed her eyes and let out a small groan. She imagined herself never experiencing these sensations again. Could she stand it?

He put the cups into position and her nipples were sucked to their fully extended position. Already she had noticed how long they were getting, more than an inch now. It would be a shame to have it all go for naught, wouldn't it?

The motor kicked in and her nipples were kneaded gently. Almost at once, she could feel her milk squirting into the tubes to gurgle into the container. "Aaahhhh," she said, feeling the beginnings of an orgasm flutter in her stomach.

Jack began to stroke her wide rump as he spoke to her. "Remember, if you stay, this will represent the dividing line between your life as a woman pretending to be a cow and your true life as a cow." His hand went down between her legs, just brushing her wet slit. "More will be required of you. You will be challenged. You will have to give yourself over to me, trust me to know what's best for you. I can assure you, I don't want any permanent harm to come to you. You're going to be my No. 1 producer. Think of the babies you'll be helping."

His voice soothed her. His hands only accentuated the feelings in her breasts and pussy. Whenever he touched her slit, she longed for him to fuck her. She imagined herself a beast, waiting to be mounted, and found the idea exciting. When he finally knelt behind her and unzipped his pants, she smiled in anticipation. No one would make love to her like Jack did. Or his friends. She had been shocked, of course, to be used like that, but she thought she could learn to accept their many favors. No pregnancy, no diseases—just a woman being fucked regularly while she gave milk. It sounded like heaven, if she could just let go of her old-fashioned morals.

She didn't know exactly what Jack had meant when he said he had a plan for her and that it might be challenging at times. She felt his cock at her entrance and pressed back to meet it. He hadn't tied her in so she could move around to show her desire for him. His cock pulled back and she knew better than to chase it. Waiting was her place in life here. She waited to be let out to pasture, waited to be milked and waited to be fucked. It would be easy to let go. She'd never have to worry about money or work or men. Since her mother had died three years ago, she was alone in the world. Why not take a little pleasure for herself?

Her orgasm built and she began to rock slightly against his cock, smearing more of her juices on the tip. She wanted to taste him, for his semen had a pleasant, salty flavor. It was funny how quickly she had gotten used to the taste of men's seed. Maybe he did know what he was doing.

He plunged into her all at once and she climaxed just as quickly, although not as powerfully as she had yesterday. Though this cock felt a little small to her now, she wasn't complaining. He pistoned inside her, and she could tell he was close. She thrust back and he leaned over her. Just as his cock erupted within her, he reached down with his right hand and found her clit and pressed it hard.

She came so hard she bucked, nearly throwing him off of her. "God! Oh GOD!" She gasped, shuddering with the power of it. "God that was good!"

When he pulled away and grabbed the cup, Brenda eagerly awaited him to finish collecting the spillage. He came around front and let her suck him off, then handed her the cup. No protein drink, she noted. At this point, she didn't care. She drank it down greedily.

"Good girl." He put the cup on the workbench, and turned to face her. "It's time for your decision. What's it going to be—stay or go?"

"Uh..." It was hard to think while her breasts were being milked like this. She thought about her life before and after meeting Jack. It had been so ordinary, so mundane. Jack represented something exciting in her life. And it satisfied a long-repressed desire. He was right—he hadn't come to her, she had come to him.

"I'll...I'll stay," she said and felt a little shudder of fear, mixed in with a delicious anticipation, once the words left her lips.

"Very well. We'll begin the next phase." He bustled about the workbench, ignoring her. She guessed she had about another ten minutes on the machine before her breasts were emptied and she couldn't imagine what he was up to. When he came forward, she spotted cordless clippers in his hand. She recoiled.

He grabbed her chin and tipped her head up. "Cows have very short hair. As a symbol of your acceptance, I'm going to trim your hair off and leave it about one-half-inch long all the way around. If you refuse, you will be sent home. If you accept your new life, you will allow me to do this."

Brenda wanted to scream, but couldn't get her vocal chords to work. She didn't move when he turned on the clippers and began shearing her like a sheep. Hair fell away in clumps and tears came to her eyes. *This is what you wanted, isn't it?* He was done about the time the bell dinged, indicating her milking was completed. She looked down to see her brown hair lying scattered on the ground. Under her hand, her scalp felt prickly.

Jack unhooked her cups and helped her stand. He rummaged in a drawer and pulled out a narrow leather belt. It clanged and she realized it had a bell attached. A cow bell. Of course. He made her raise her chin and fastened it around her neck. The bell lay between her collarbones. "Now I'll be able to hear you wherever you go. And when you are being fucked, it will make a delightful noise."

He made her drop to all fours as he brought her outside and proceeded to hose her down thoroughly. Brenda was thankful to be clean—she had lost track of how many days she had wallowed in the dirt and dust. After allowing her body to air dry, he brought her back inside. Pointing to the workbench, had her hoist herself up on it, and lay back. Her pussy was exposed to him. She feared what else he might do.

"Finally, I want to do one more thing." He tugged at the brown fleece between her legs. "This has got to go. I realize cows are covered in fur, but since you have none, I want you entirely naked, except for your head. We're going to remove it."

She thought he would simply shave it, but he had other plans. He took out a box and showed her the label. "Wax-Off Permanent Hair Removal" it said. She gasped. "That's going to hurt!"

"Yes it will. But no more than the spankings you've been given lately. If you'd like, I could call Charlie and some other guys over to help hold you down."

"Uh, no, that's okay." She gritted her teeth and tried to think about all the women who paid hundreds of dollars to have this procedure done in beauty salons across the country. Jack heated up the wax packet by waving a blowtorch under it, then cut off a corner and began smearing the warm solution over her mons. Before it set, he pressed a strip of cloth over it. He waited a minute, then yanked it hard, causing Brenda to cry out, jerking her legs in protest.

"Ow! Dammit! That hurts!"

"Looks good. See? He held up the furry strip. She glanced down to see a pale stripe of skin at the top of her mound. "Only a few more to go."

She gritted her teeth as he laid down a second strip and yanked it free. "Jesus! I think I'd rather be whipped!"

"One more here, then we can get the smaller hairs along both sides."

Brenda groaned, but didn't fight him as he completed the process. When he was finished, he held up a mirror so she could see. Her genitals were very sore and red, but all the hair was gone, even down to her asshole.

Jack took out a small tube. "Now this is to prevent the hair from returning. We wouldn't want to have to continue waxing, would we?"

"No way."

The cream actually felt good as he put it on. In fact, it made her wet all over again. Then it began to burn. "Ouch! It's getting hot! Take it off!" Her bell clanged.

Jack was reading the label. "Yes, it says that it will get warm. But we have to leave it on twenty minutes for it to work."

She jerked and gasped, but endured it to the end, feeling like she'd leaned up against a stove. Finally, he took her outside and rinsed off her genitals with the hose. She looked down—her cunt had turned an angry shade of red. "Is it supposed to look like this?"

"Yes, just for another twelve hours. Then it should fade back to normal."

"God." She touched her hair. "I must look like a freak."

"No, you look more like a cow. It pleases me. Now, for your new name."

"New name? What's wrong with Brenda?"

"I've never seen a cow named Brenda. I'm going to call you Bessie."

Brenda thought about objecting, but the truth was, she rather liked it in an odd sort of way. One of the cows in the dairy barn she had visited so long ago had been named Bessie. She had to admit, it did make her feel more like a cow. And with her heavy breasts, she was becoming quite the milk producer.

The next day, her period started, disappointing and embarrassing her. She hid in her stall, ashamed to come out due to the blood that seeped out of her. When Master showed up, she asked him for a pad, but he just laughed.

"Cows don't wear pads."

"But I'll bleed all over everything! And the flies are terrible!"

"You'll get used to it."

She hated him right then. How could he be so cruel? She smelled bad and the flies wouldn't leave her alone. He even put her into the machine like this, her blood dripping down both thighs. Fortunately, no one wanted to fuck her during those times!

The next few days passed in a blur. Her period finally ended, thank god, and he hosed her down so she felt a little more normal. But her training never abated. There were more rules, more swats with the crop when she disobeyed or talked back. But her milk production continued to increase and she always had those wonderful orgasms. Charlie was still her No. 1 man, with his large cock that fit her so well, but she quickly learned to appreciate the others. She never did learn their names. She only saw their faces when they presented their wet cocks for her to clean. Some were tall, some short, some ugly. They all fucked her with a casual disregard.

Brenda—no, Bessie now—found her life ruled more and more by her tits and cunt. She had to be milked every morning and evening, or her breasts would ache terribly. And she knew, every time she was on the machine, she could count on someone to fuck her silly. She let herself go and learned to become more like an animal, and not try to think about her life too much.

One day, during an afternoon milking, after Charlie had just given her a soul-wrenching orgasm and she was busy sucking him off, she felt another cock at her back and tipped her hips up to accept it, like normal. But this cock felt different, somehow. For one, it was bigger, but it also felt cooler. She turned and looked over her shoulder and got the shock of her life.

Kneeling there was a large woman with heavy breasts encased in a black sports bra, but naked from the waist down. Her hair was cropped into a butch and she had a smug expression on her face. Attached to her mons was a rubber dildo in the shape of a man's cock that even now was bumping up against her. But it was like nothing she had ever seen before. It was even larger than Charlie's! "Hey," she started and Jack struck her with the riding crop at once.

"This is part of your training," he warned.

"But she's too—"

Whap! Whap!

"You're big enough. Don't worry. I won't let you get hurt."

The woman pressed forward and Bessie felt the cock part her nether lips. She sucked in her breath. It stretched the walls of her pussy as it slid in. The woman was being gentle, thank god for that, she thought. But she was also relentless. She kept pressing, pulling back a little to spread the wetness, then pressing it in again. Within a few minutes, she had thrust it all inside.

"Oh, my god!" Bessie had never felt so full. She worried she would get all stretched out so Jack's cock would flop around inside like a pencil in a tin can. Heck, even Charlie's would feel a bit small in comparison! The woman pulled it back out and Bessie thought her insides might go with her. "Ohhhhh, goooooooood," she muttered.

The woman pressed it in again, then back out. Each time she moved a little faster. Her bell clanged out the rhythm. Despite the fullness, Bessie felt an orgasm approach. "Oh, yeah, baby, oh yeah," she encouraged her.

The woman knew what she was doing. Back and forth that huge cock plunged, rubbing her in areas she'd never been touched before. She soon forgot it was a woman with a strap-on behind her and got into the rhythm of the fucking.

She felt her orgasm approach quickly, then wash over her. But the woman never slowed down. Another climax, then a third—still the woman fucked her. Bessie realized that without the ability to climax herself, the woman could go as long as her muscles held out.

Her orgasms began to overlap, her brain fogged. Still the woman kept pistoning into her. "Stop, stop, stop," she begged, helpless before the onslaught. When she doubted she could climax any more, the woman suddenly leaned over her, reached underneath and pinched her swollen clit hard between her fingers. It triggered a final, explosive orgasm that left her limp. The woman pulled the dildo out with a "plop."

"Thanks, Agnes," Jack said.

"Anytime."

Agnes came around to present the rubber cock to Bessie's face and she grimaced, but didn't protest. It was too large to take inside, so she licked it clean from the outside. Agnes smiled and patted her on the head and went to a corner to dress.

"Why did you do that to me?" Bessie asked Jack, her voice showing her hurt.

"I wanted you to experience a nice large cock. And Agnes here really wanted to fuck you."

"Charlie's cock is big enough for me."

"Not for me. I like to see you push yourself."

Bessie's cunt ached. "Well, I've been pushed. Can't say that I liked it."

"It appeared that you did. You came several times."

She shrugged. "I guess."

"Don't worry, you'll get used to it." His words chilled her.

CHAPTER SIX

The hot summer days crawled by. After that last washing, Bessie had been left to the dirt and it now nearly covered her body. Flies buzzed around her and she spent a lot of her free time brushing them off. As Jack had promised, Agnes became a regular part of Bessie's afternoon milking sessions. She was glad it was just once a day, for she doubted she could've handled that large dildo both morning and afternoon. In the morning, she would fuck Charlie or some of the other men and she found she really enjoyed those sessions.

But in the afternoon, her cunt belonged to Agnes, who was no longer silent about it. She made it clear she was a butch lesbian who enjoyed fucking and humiliating Bessie. To her chagrin, Bessie always came hard on the huge rubber cock, leaving her limp and shaking.

"Come on, dirty cow, open that cunt up for me," Agnes would tell her as she thrust her tool into the helpless woman. "You know you love it. Tell me you love my cock."

She would pound her until Bessie would tell her anything to make her stop. "I love it! I love it! I love your big cock!"

"Tell me you're my bitch!"

"I'm your bitch!"

Jack would film their sessions to record her humiliation. He brought in a flat-screen monitor and a DVD player and showed Bessie some of his edited films of her with Agnes or Charlie or the line of men. The movies only added to her embarrassment. Seeing the dirt on her large body, how she begged to be fucked, or the way her cowbell rang out each thrust. She saw herself as the others saw her now—an animal, a cow, a thing.

Within two weeks, Bessie had grown accustomed to the large dildo until even Charlie's cock began to feel small to her. She cried when she realized that, for she had enjoyed their sessions so much. Now she began to look forward to Agnes' visits, for her cunt had come to welcome the large cock inside her, filling her up. Her only regret was that it never came inside her. She missed the sensation of a man's cock erupting into her womb, even if she couldn't get pregnant.

She tried to question Jack about why he was allowing Agnes to stretch her out, but he was enigmatic about it. She persisted, until one day when he let her out in the morning, he didn't take her right to the machine. Instead, he brought her over to the workbench and made her squat on her haunches at his feet. Her breasts ached with a need to be milked, but she was curious about this change in routine.

"We need to talk about the new rules."

"More new rules?"

"Yes. For one, I no longer want to hear you talk. After all, cows don't talk."

Bessie's mouth dropped open.

"I realize you might have some urgent news to give me now and again, but I'm going to begin training you not to speak," Jack continued. "You may make guttural noises, of course, or say 'mooo,' but human speech will have consequences."

"C-consequences? What kind of consequences?'"

"For every word you speak, you will be given one swat with the riding crop or the dressage whip."

She had seen the riding crop. It wasn't so bad. In fact, she had rather grown to like how it heated up her ass prior to a good fucking. "What's a dressage whip?"

"I'll show you." He reached around. Leaning up against the workbench was a five-foot leather whip, about as thick as a man's finger at one end and tapering down to a thin whippy end, culminating in a tassel.

"Oh, god."

"That's ten."

"What?"

"That's eleven strokes with this."

"No way!"

"Thirteen."

Her mouth came open, then shut. She shook her head.

He smiled. "Since this is your first time, I'll just give you one, so you can feel what it's like."

He made her turn around and grip the bench. She didn't know why she did it, except that she thought one stroke was a heck of a lot better than thirteen. He touched her inner thighs, making her open her legs more. She felt so exposed there and at his mercy. He stepped back to her side. She braced herself.

SHHH-WHAAP!

"SHIT!" The whip laid fire across her wide rump. She jumped up and grabbed her ass with both hands, hopping about the room and yelping. Her bell clanged noisily.

"Stings, doesn't it?"

"You bastard! You can't hit me with that! I'll quit!"

"You can't quit. You belong to me now. And that's eleven more for real this time."

She shook her head angrily. God, she'd been such a fool! Why hadn't she just left? Would it have been so bad to go home and return to her normal life? She wanted to ask him how he thought he could keep her here against her will. She realized, too late, that this is what Jack had been talking about when he had said she had reached the dividing line a few weeks ago. She had assumed that she could still leave, if she wanted to. Now she knew that he meant to keep her forever—but more importantly, she would let him. For she had gone too far to go back now and she knew it.

Jack continued, his voice patient and calm, as if he was addressing a child. "However, I will allow you one word for free. It's the word that will use to call me from now on. The word is 'Master.'"

Bessie paled. This was going far beyond her desire to be a cow, she realized. He was making her his total submissive. "Master?" she said, trying the word out for the first time.

"That's right. If you have a question to ask, start with 'Master.' Every other word will result in a stroke of the whip or crop, so choose your words carefully."

Bessie hoped he would choose the crop over the whip. That thing hurt! She rubbed her ass and thought about how narrow her life was becoming. Even if she wasn't well-bathed, she was well-fed, well-milked and well-fucked, and that was the sum total of her life. She had to obey Jack—or Master—without question.

It was no longer a game.

He led her back to the machine and tied her to the frame. Her heart pounded. Her tits ached to be drained, yet she feared the whip. The pain, the dirt, her predicament faded in importance to her immediate need. She watched Master get into position.

WHAP!

She sucked in her breath. Though it hurt, he hadn't hit her nearly as hard as he had the first time.

WHAP! WHAP! Bessie endured the remaining blows, her ass quaking with every strike. She knew he was holding back and wondered why. Did he not want to sour her milk?

"There," he said when he finished. "Next time, I'll hit harder." She looked over her shoulder at the red marks and shuddered to think how much pain the whip could produce if he desired it.

She was filthy, so it took longer than normal for Master to clean off her breasts. She waited patiently, without a word. He held up the electrolyte mixture and she gulped it down. Finally, he attached the cups and began the long process of milking her. She sighed contentedly.

She heard the shuffle of feet and didn't bother to look around as a man's cock plunged into her. She recognized Charlie at once. When he climaxed, after giving her a quick orgasm herself, she was surprised and a bit disappointed to realize that he was alone. She looked questioningly at Master, but his face told her nothing.

The rest of the day she lolled about the pasture, nibbling on the food Master had brought her and lapping up water from the trough that he always kept full. He had always encouraged her to drink plenty of water.

When five o'clock came, she felt that familiar heaviness in her breasts and eagerly awaited her Master. He came about fifteen minutes later and led her back into the barn. She was happy to follow. After she was watered and cleaned off, Master announced: "Agnes is here."

Bessie's cunt twitched and she turned to look back. It surprised her how much she had started to look forward to these sessions. The back door opened and Bessie saw her saunter in, dressed in a black sports bra and huge dildo, as usual.

Agnes approached and got down on her knees behind Bessie. The cock spread her labia and began to work its way inside. "Take it bitch. You know your cunt can handle it," Agnes sneered.

"Oh god," Bessie breathed, already feeling her cunt expand around it.

Jack waggled a finger at her and shook his head.

Agnes worked the cock inside, inch by inch, but her cunt by now could accept it. Bessie groaned with pleasure. Sweat poured off her body. She looked up at one point to see Master with his video camera, recording her humiliation. She was sure she'd be seeing that tape many times.

Finally, the dildo hit bottom. It always made Bessie feel like she was riding a fence post. When Agnes began to pull out, Bessie thought she was being turned inside out. Her bell clanged loudly.

"Noooo," she groaned.

Master came close to film how the dildo entered her, her cunt stretched around it like a balloon. Then he reached out and flicked Bessie's clit that was fully extended and she shuddered with the sensations that rocked her. As the cock pistoned into her, she felt the first flutterings of an orgasm. Master again brushed her clit and her body responded. "Master," she breathed, encouraging him without risking another whipping.

He kept the camera close, occasionally reaching in to touch her clit or smear her juices around the dildo. It definitely felt good now and Bessie imagined a climax was possible. Agnes, as usual, was tireless, pounding her hips up against Bessie's wide ass, making sure that cock hit bottom.

"Ah, ah, ah," Bessie said, announcing that she was close. She was thrusting back now, encouraging Agnes. "Gah, gah, gah, gah," she vocalized, feeling the wave beginning to crest inside of her.

Agnes kept up the pressure until Bessie hung on the edge, waiting to be pushed over. Master pinched her clit and that did it. "Aaaaggggghhhh!" she screamed. Agnes pushed the dildo deep inside her and Bessie wished for the umpteenth time that this rubber cock could squirt inside her like Charlie's and the others' did. Still, she managed a second orgasm. Then Master pinched her clit again, triggering a third. Agnes wasn't done—she kept up the pressure, making Bessie helpless against the assaults.

When they finally let her go, Bessie had lost count of the climaxes she had experienced. "God," she breathed, falling limp to the mat. Agnes pulled out, leaving her cunt gaping open.

Agnes came forward and made her clean off the cock. It was like cleaning off a telephone pole with her tongue. When she was done, Agnes stripped off the dildo and held it on one hand, then moved her body up against Bessie's, her cunt just inches from her face. "Bring me off, slut," she commanded. Bessie looked over at Master, who nodded. He brushed her sore rump with the whip.

She had never made love to a woman before, but she did that morning. Bessie licked and sucked the large woman's pussy and clit like she was an expert. It took a long time and all the while, flies buzzed around her open cunt and Master stroked her body with the tip of the whip, encouraging her.

At last, Agnes cried out and pressed Bessie's head tightly against her pussy, cutting off her air. She didn't release her until Bessie had begun seeing spots before her eyes. She gasped for breath. Agnes smiled and winked and said, "You'll make a great cunt-licker with some practice."

Bessie didn't like the sound of that.

Master unzipped his pants and announced, "This should make up for the lack of sperm," and thrust his cock into her mouth. Bessie sucked it down and soon brought him to a climax, tasting his salty cum on her tongue.

CHAPTER SEVEN

She was left alone in the pasture for the rest of the afternoon and well into the evening. She liked it after dark, for the heat of the day finally ebbed and the night breezes blew. Master brought her out some dinner—a roast beef sandwich that he fed to her, since her hands were filthy—and made sure she had plenty of water. Her cunt still ached, as it always did after a session with Agnes, but she was otherwise content.

Later that evening, Master led her into her stall, her cowbell announcing her movements. She lay down on her dirty blanket and soon fell asleep.

In the morning, Master milked her, as usual, but no one showed up to fuck her. That was very odd. She had always been fucked while she milked. What went wrong? She stamped her hands and shook her ass to show her displeasure, but Master ignored her. She almost talked to him, but decided to wait and see what happened.

When she was led to the pasture, Bessie was still horny. She had grown used to the constant fucking and didn't like to do without. She thought she might wait until he left, then give herself a quick orgasm. But, as usual, Master had guessed how she felt. He fastened leather bracelets to her wrists and attached them with short lengths of chain to her collar. She could kneel on her hands and knees, as usual, but the chains were too short to allow either hand to reach her pussy.

Frustrated, she slumped down in the grass and waited. She knew something was brewing and wasn't sure how she felt about it.

By the time five o'clock came, she was beside herself with curiosity. When he called for her, she came bouncing up, as fast as the chains on her wrists would allow. He unhooked them immediately and removed the bracelets.

Inside, she went to the machine and waited, but he shook his head. "I've got another surprise for you. A new milking machine!"

He made it sound exciting, so she smiled and nodded her head in agreement. He slapped his thigh, indicating she should come along, and moved toward the back of the barn. She had never been beyond the double doors, so she was naturally curious to see what lay beyond.

When he opened the doors, Bessie found herself in another part of the barn, equal in size to the one she had been in for three months. The stalls seemed bigger, but otherwise, the rooms looked a lot alike. But it was the large machine in the middle that drew her attention. That it was a milking machine, Bessie had no doubt, for she could see the cups below and the tubes leading away. But the wooden frame was much larger compared to the other one. Inside, there were padded areas and dowels and all sorts of strange angles. She couldn't understand it. Why did it have to be so big? Had she gotten too fat for the other one?

"Come on, I'll show you how it works. I just finished it a while ago."

She approached cautiously. He helped her climb into it and showed her how her hips set against the padded bench and her hands gripped the dowels in front while she got into place. Then her feet and hands went into boots and gloves and she was strapped in, unable to move. Another pad braced her shoulders. Her ass was up and her legs were held shoulder's width apart. She found once she had her body in position, it was more comfortable. Only her heavy breasts hung free. Suddenly, it became clear. Her open pussy was displayed at cock height. This was to make it easier for her "lovers"—they would no longer have to kneel behind her. She breathed a sigh of relief. She had been afraid there would be something more sinister to it.

Jack cleaned off her breasts and attached the cups. The milking, at least seemed familiar. She settled in, listening to the hum of the machinery, lulled into complacency. It was nice to be off her hands and knees, she decided.

She heard a noise and turned to see Master opening the rear door, which led outside. He whistled and she felt a pang of fear. What was he calling? And why? She felt she already knew the answer to that. Alarmed, she tried to shift her position so she could see better, but she was well secured.

The noises behind her caused her cunt and asshole to pucker up, but exposed as she was, she knew whatever it was would have complete access to her. *My god*, she suddenly thought. *I'm supposed to be a cow—he can't possibly mean to mate me with a bull!*

As if in response, Master called to someone, "Here, Bull, look what I've got for ya!"

"Nooo!" She screamed, struggling helplessly.

Master gave a swat on her rump with the whip, burning a line of fire. "Is that any way to treat your mate?" He demanded.

She felt hands on her ass and thought Master was helping the bull get into position. This can't be happening! "Noooo!" She shrieked again, not afraid of the whip any longer. She didn't want to be fucked by a bull!

The smell of an overripe body struck her and she gasped, just as the prod of a cock at her slit sent her shaking in her bonds, trying to avoid it. Then the cock slipped in a ways and she grew still. Her brow furrowed. Though large, it felt very familiar. Then she realized where she had felt such a cock before. Agnes! He had been kidding her! It was only Agnes behind her!

Except it didn't feel exactly like Agnes' rubber cock. The size was right, but not the shape. And this one was warm, not cool like hers was. "What's happening?" she asked.

The cock slipped fully inside now. God he was big!

She heard a guttural sound and feared what strange beast might be back there, fucking her while she was helpless. Then the cock began to move and she relaxed a little and stopped trying to fight it. It did no good anyway.

The sensations increased and she found her cunt could handle the monster within her. Now she understood why Master had Agnes use the strap-on—no man was large enough. Charlie was close, but this cock in her was huge!

She groaned as she felt the orgasm approach. "Yes, fuck me," she breathed, falling into the rhythms of her body and letting her mind drift. She knew she was talking too much and there would be punishment later for it, but she didn't care. Her world consisted of this cock, her cunt—and of course, her tits being gently milked.

The orgasm erupted within her and she cried out, but the cock did not stop pumping. She came again and again and began to wonder if this beast fucking her was human or some hybrid superman, bred to fuck. The only sounds she could hear were the slap of his flesh against her buttocks and an odd grunting noise he made.

Suddenly, her erupted within her and she felt the sperm splash inside. This triggered yet another climax and she passed out for a moment. When she came to, Master was patting her on her shoulder and telling her how proud he was of her. He held up a cup for her and she drank down the sperm mixture that had seeped from her cunt.

She couldn't stop herself from asking: "Who was that?"

Master sighed. "That was my son." He didn't seem to mind that she was talking again.

Bessie was shocked. "Your son?"

He nodded. "He's, um, special. He became trapped in his mother's birth canal and they had to perform an emergency C-section on her." He paused. "She didn't survive. And he was born somewhat brain-damaged."

"I'm sorry to hear that," she said. "I didn't know you had a son. I've never seen him before."

"He lives in the tack room in the barn and hangs out in the back pasture a lot. He's, uh, not comfortable around most people. He prefers it out here with the animals. He's pretty good with them."

"You called him Bull. Is that a nickname or something?"

"Yes. He's really Jack Jr., but he was so big and strong growing up, I just started calling him Bull."

Suddenly, Bessie understood. "So that's what this has been about. You didn't want to help me live out my fantasies as much as you wanted a fucktoy for your son, right?"

He frowned. "I wouldn't call you a fucktoy. More like a mate."

She remembered now that he had called her that before, while his son was fucking her. Her blood ran cold. "You can't mean…"

"Oh yes. He's going to get you pregnant. I'm taking you off the birth control."

"No! You can't!"

"Of course you can. I own you now—you're my cow, remember?"

"I can't be a mom and a cow too!"

"Oh, you won't be a real mom. Just a breeder. I'll raise the babies. Me and my girlfriend."

"Babies!" In her mind, she shouted: *Girlfriend!?*

"Yes. I don't know how many yet. But it won't matter to you. You'll be well taken care of."

"Why have your son fuck me—why not fuck me yourself?"

"Two reasons. My girlfriend objects to me fucking you, for obvious reasons, and I wanted my son to experience it. And he's the next closest thing to me."

"Aren't you worried that the babies might be born, um, damaged?"

"No!" Anger flickered across his face. "His oxygen was cut off. He doesn't have bad genes. And you've talked too much. I've been too lenient. It's time for some punishment."

"Wait!"

He paused.

"Can I meet him?"

Master pursed his lips. "He can't really talk well. I can understand him some, but you won't be able to."

"Still, he fucked me. I'd like to see him."

Master nodded and looked behind her. "He's sitting over there, watching you. I'll see if I can get him to come over."

He disappeared from view. Bessie waited patiently, her heart pounding. She could hear the flies buzzing around her, occasionally landing to drink of her fluids. She contracted her pussy and shook them off.

A shuffling noise came. Bessie tried not to appear threatening. Of course, considering she was still trapping in the frame, being milked, should eliminate any worries Bull might have. Master came into view, talking softly to a man he held by his arm, gently encouraging him.

"Here she is, Bull. This is your new girlfriend. Isn't she pretty?"

"Ughhnneed," the man said.

Bessie turned her head to get a better look. Her eyes widened. Bull was naked and filthy—just like her. He was a large man in his early twenties. She thought he might stand six-six or six-seven and had a broad chest like his father, except his stomach was rounder, typical of a man who didn't exercise. Below his belly, his cock, though flaccid now, appeared enormous. She raised her eyes to his face, taking in his shaggy hair and a wispy beard. What really struck Bessie was his expression. Mostly blank, but with some curiosity behind the eyes. He kept his eyes down for the most part, glancing up as if to catch sight of her only in small doses.

She was to be this man's mate, possibly for the rest of her life.

She tried to smile, but her heart wasn't in it. She had been a fool. While she thought Jack's master plan was all about her desire to be milked like a cow, it really was all about his son. *He's pretty good with animals*, Master had said. So he went out and found himself a human animal for him. And she had fallen right into his trap.

"Let me out!" she demanded. Bull recoiled.

Master's voice darkened. "You're scaring him. You'll be sorry for that."

He turned to Bull. "Are you all right?"

Bull made some guttural noise and Master nodded. "Very well. Why don't you stand over there and watch? I'll make her behave."

Bessie's heart fell. She knew what was coming. "Master—"

"Too late," he growled. He picked up the dressage whip. She could feel her asshole contract.

WHAP! "Aaeeiih!" He hit her so hard! She shook in the frame.

WHAP! WHAP! Again on the same cheek—the left one. She didn't understand—why not switch to give her sore flesh a rest?

"Please!"

Twice more he struck her on the same side, then, strangely, he stopped. Behind her, Bessie could hear Bull's voice. She couldn't understand the words, but she could tell he was coming to her aid, asking Master to stop.

"Okay, okay, Bull. But I have to train her, you understand?"

There were more vocalizations, and Master appeared by her head. "You're a fortunate cow. Bull says you've had enough. I hope you appreciate it."

She nodded vigorously. She tried to crane her neck to smile at Bull, but he hung back, out of sight.

Master looked back. "It's time to heat up the branding iron, son. You remember how to do that?"

Branding iron!

Bull came forward then, nodding, his face coming to life. "Brinnndggg." He moved off.

"No! Don't do this! I'll be good, I promise!"

"Too late. Besides, this is something Bull understands. He's been helping me take care of the cows and he's been branding them for a few years now. Actually, you see..." He stopped, his head cocked to one side, as if trying to decide if he should tell her. "Well, I guess it won't matter if you know. You see, I got the idea to have a human cow when I came into the barn one day and found Bull fucking one of the young heifers. I was shocked, but I quickly realized it was only instinct. And since he could never get a regular woman, I thought a woman who had a strong desire to be a cow would be perfect for him."

"Noooo!"

"You were perfect. You really got into this whole cow lifestyle. And now, even if you could, I'll bet you wouldn't want to quit. For what I told you earlier is still true—you can't satisfy your inner desires anywhere else but here. And you satisfy mine for my son."

"Please don't brand me!"

"You don't understand. By putting his brand on you, he'll make you his. In his limited understanding, he'll feel you're his property. He'll be able to trust you more and bring you into his little world. He's got no one else but me, you know."

"Please! I'll be his friend! I don't want to be branded!" Now she knew why her right buttock had remained unmarked by the whip.

"But of course you do. It's one of the final acts of being a cow. Look at you, you're being milked twice a day and every time, you've had your ass up to be fucked by strangers. Even by a bull dyke." He chuckled at the cow reference. "Once you are branded, you can allow yourself to become the cow you've always wanted to be, deep down."

The bell dinged at that moment, indicating her milking was finished for the day. Master came forward and unhooked the cups from her empty breasts. She was distracted for a moment, then something he had said came back to her.

"One of the final acts?"

He grinned. "We're not done. There will be a few other modifications."

"God no! I want to go home!"

"You are home."

He left her there, sobbing in the frame, struggling against her bonds. She could hear them in the background, moving around. The smell of burning coal soon filled the barn. Master came forward and washed off her right buttock. She cried and pleaded to no avail until her voice failed her. At one point, Master told her she would have to be punished, later, for all her talking.

"Oh, god, noooo!"

"Don't move," she heard after a while and she braced herself. The white-hot sear of pain stabbed at her right buttock. "Aaaaaaaggghhhhh!" she screamed.

The fire went away, but the pain remained, then seemed to blossom. Cool water was splashed on her rump and it soothed her just for a moment. More water was poured and she cried and babbled her pain. Someone came forward and rubbed some soothing lotion on her, easing the pain somewhat. She was grateful for this little bit of kindness.

They finally let her out of the machine. Bessie could barely move. She looked at once at the painful brand and saw it was a capital B in a circle. The B could stand for Bessie, but she knew it was for Bull. The son smiled at her and patted her side, like one might pet a dog. His eyes lit up when he saw the brand.

"Yes, she's all yours now, Bull. Take good care of her."

"Mnnnngh."

"Oh god," she moaned.

"And if she continues to talk, perhaps we can remove her vocal chords," Master added, looking meaningfully at her.

She opened her mouth to protest, and realized that would not be the smart thing to do. She decided not to risk it and simply shook her head. Master laughed.

CHAPTER EIGHT

That was the beginning of the final stage in her strange new life. She was carefully monitored now and whenever she was left alone at night, she was chained up, like a beast. They wouldn't let her go, ever.

Bull fucked her twice a day during her milkings. Surprisingly, she got used to his smell. She imagined she didn't smell much better. Her cunt easily accommodated his large cock. If she climaxed, fine, but if not, too bad. Sometimes he'd come into her stall at night to have at her. She tried to refuse him, just once. In her milking frame, she was helpless, but in her own stall, she had felt some indignity at being interrupted during sleep and had pushed him off. He didn't force himself on her, but his expression was one of hurt and confusion. He had left, muttering to himself.

The next morning, she learned the price for her disobedience. Master came in, furious. Bessie wasn't sure how Bull conveyed her resistance, but it was clear he knew. Perhaps he had seen it on the video camera.

"You NEVER refuse him! Never!" She realized she was in a lot of trouble and tried to get away. Both men dragged her to the heavy frame and strapped her in. Her ass was always presented so invitingly up in this way. Master stepped back and struck her several times with the whip, causing her to cry and beg for forgiveness.

He gave the whip to Bull. Surprisingly, he didn't strike her as hard, for which she was grateful. Afterwards, he fucked her in the frame, his groin pounding hard against her sore rump until tears blurred her vision.

During the entire time, she wasn't milked. Her breasts ached. Master came forward with the cup of Bull's sperm, as usual and held it up for her. She thought about refusing, but realized that would only cause him to whip her more. She drank it down quickly.

"I want you to think about your position here. You are a cow, nothing more. You are her to obey. If my son wants to fuck you, day or night, you let him. In exchange, we will relieve the pain of your swollen breasts. To show you just how dependent you are on us, I'm not going to milk you this morning. Your breasts will swell to the breaking point. You will be in agony by noon."

He paused and Bessie realized he was right. As long as she was milked regularly, she felt somewhat normal. Take away the milkings and she would quickly find out how dependant she was on them.

"Please," she said and he struck her with the whip again.

"I don't want to hear your voice again. For now, I'm going to gag you so you can't talk. Don't make me remove your vocal chords." He went to the workbench and returned with a ball gag that he worked in between her teeth and fastened behind her neck. He showed her a small padlock so she'd know she couldn't remove it herself and she heard it click into place. The rubber ball tasted new and it was quite bitter. She hated it at once.

He unfastened her and helped her from the frame. "Now get out," he snarled and pointed toward the front doors. She meekly crawled out to the pasture, followed by Bull. She knew why he was there. Her breasts ached as he fucked her from behind, her head forced down into the short grass. They continued to ache as he turned her over and fucked her on her back, his overpowering smell washing over her and her bell clanging out their rhythms. He came inside her twice and she knew she would get pregnant soon. Then her breasts would swell even more, demanding that she expel more of her milk regularly.

She was in a vicious cycle from which there was no escape.

After Bull left her alone, she lay in the grass, trying to ignore the pain of her swollen breasts. This was a very effective punishment, she realized. She'd be willing to do just about anything to avoid a repeat of his pain.

By noon, she was gasping through her nose. Her breasts felt like twin balloons that had been overfilled. Her nipples leaked milk into the grass and she tried to milk herself in secret, hoping that Master or Bull wouldn't catch her. But she could only squeeze out a few drops and that was far from adequate.

With the gag in, she couldn't drink or eat, and the hot sun seemed to suck the juices out of her. She thought perhaps that would help dry up her milk, but no such luck. If anything, her breasts were sucking all the remaining fluids from her body.

Another hour or two had passed before Master returned, a naked Bull right behind him. She could see he was excited, for his cock was half-hard and rising fast at the sight of her. Bessie gasped out her relief when he motioned for her to come to the barn. She moved as fast as her swollen tits would allow.

Inside, it was marginally cooler and she waited to be put into the machine. Master came forward and removed the gag, then gave her a big glass of water. She gulped it down quickly.

"I'm going to let you speak, one last time," he said. "After today, I don't want to hear anything or you will be punished double. Do you understand?"

She nodded, afraid to speak. She could only wait for the milking to begin.

"Good. Now I know your breasts hurt terribly. And I'm sure you realize now how much you need these milkings."

She nodded again.

"I'll put you in the machine and milk you until you are empty— but first, you have to beg me to put in a ring in your nose."

"What!? A ring?" She could visualize it at once—a big steel ring, just like a cow might wear. It would go perfectly with the damn bell she's always wearing. "Oh, god!"

"If you refuse, we'll take you back to the pasture."

"No! Not that! Okay, but please, can you do it so it won't hurt so much?"

"No," he said simply. "But I will make you a compromise. I'll start your milking first."

"Yes! Please!"

He helped her climb into the machine and she was soon securely fastened. Her chin rested on the padded bench and she knew her nose was about to be violated. Strangely, as soon as Master hooked up her tits, her mind went into its stupor and she relaxed. "Aaaaaah," she breathed.

Master came forward, with Bull standing right next to him, watching. Master smeared some sort of salve on both sides of her septum, and took out a tool she had never seen before. He placed the tip inside her nostrils and she braced herself for the pain. He clamped down and the pain shot through her face as if she'd been punched. Her eyes watered and blood flowed down her lip and into her mouth.

"Aaaaaaagh!"

He removed the tool and smeared a salve on the wound to slow the bleeding. Then he threaded a heavy steel ring through the hole that hung down over her upper lip. It tugged at her wound, making her cry harder.

"The salve I put on there should stop the bleeding and ease the pain. But it will take a week or so to fully heal. We won't use it until then."

Her face settled into a dull throb and she was grateful that, for once, Bull wasn't fucking her. The pounding action would only exacerbate her pain. They left her there, the pain slowly fading as the pleasure of her breasts increased. Flies buzzed around her, but she made no effort to shake them off.

It took a long time for her tits to be emptied. Finally, the bell dinged and the machine shut off automatically. Bessie lay there another half-hour before Master returned.

"All done, I see. I'll let you out for a while. Here, let me check your nose first." He peered at the ring and the way it seated itself in her septum and announced himself satisfied.

Bessie was left alone until after seven, when Master brought her some dinner and gave her another quick milking to hold her over during the long night. She appreciated this little bit of kindness and even smiled at him when he placed her in the machine.

She was learning.

Bull came up behind her and started fucking her. The pain in her nose increased, but she ignored it and tried to squeeze his cock with her pussy to make him come more quickly. Her bell clanged. When he squirted into her, she sank down happily. By now, Master had added a small bucket underneath her spread legs and she could hear the semen splash into it. Bull brought it around for her to drink and she did, without argument. He patted her on the shoulder.

"Guddd grrrr."

She smiled wanly. She was beginning to understand his strange speech. Another measure of how she was truly becoming his.

For the next week, they left her nose ring alone. She was still milked twice a day and fucked regularly by Bull, but otherwise, her life had become routine. When her nose healed, they began clipping the leash to it to bring her out to pasture or back to the barn. Bessie followed along willingly out of fear that her nose would be damaged if she didn't.

The next day, a stranger appeared with Master at her stall. He was short and had tattoos up and down both arms. Bessie cringed down into her blanket until Master snapped his fingers and ordered her to show her body. They talked about her as if she couldn't understand English.

"That's her. What do you think?"

"Hmm. She's got a lot to work with. I suggest a two-stage process."

"What do you mean?"

"Let's start with a dye at first. It's like henna, only darker."

Bessie felt her hair and wondered why they'd want to dye it. What was wrong with it?

The stranger continued. "Then, if you like it, we can make it permanent."

Master nodded. "Okay. Go ahead."

He took her outside and washed her off. When she was led back to the heavy frame, the stranger was waiting nearby. Bessie didn't like that, but she no longer had any control over her life. When she was strapped in and helpless, the stranger approached with a small can and a brush. What the hell was he doing?

He began to paint large sections of her body with the dye. She could only see him in the camera screen for she could not turn her head. Bessie watched, baffled. The paint tingled a little and she squirmed in the frame. Master, as usual, gave her a warning slap with the riding crop.

It took awhile before she understood what the man was doing. He was painting large dark splotches on her like a cow! What were those kind called? She remembered seeing them at the dairy farm, so many years ago. Oh yes, Holsteins. Master wanted her to look like a Holstein.

The man finished by painting part of her face with the dye. She could see how it made her look unhuman. More cowlike. As a reward, Master allowed him to fuck her. His cock was small and she didn't come like she did with Bull. When he stepped away and came into her range of vision, she was surprised to see that he had worn a condom. How nice. Master was saving her for his son. Of course, that didn't stop him from making her drink the semen from the used rubber.

Her dye job seemed to please Master. It faded after a week and he brought the stranger back to make it permanent. She really tried to fight them, then, but it did no good. Master waited until she was in the frame, helpless, before the tattoo artist appeared. She struggled and protested, and was rewarded with a dozen sharp cracks with the dressage whip.

When he started on her rump, she gave up and stopped struggling, even though the needle stung her. To make it easier on her, Master gently stroked her cunt while the man worked, but stopped before she came. After an hour of being denied, Bessie was beside herself and the tattooing only seemed like a minor buzzing compared to her unmet need.

"That's enough for today," the man said and Master again let him fuck her when he had put away his equipment.

He returned every few days for the next two weeks, each time adding more ink to her skin until she really did begin to look like a Holstein, with those large dark splotches randomly placed. The transformation cemented her life as a cow. She could never go back. When she was alone in her stall, she cried.

CHAPTER NINE

The air was becoming cooler now during the night. She realized that she had been here four months. Her tattooing was complete and she couldn't bear to look at herself in the video screen. Half her face was darkened by a rounded pattern, like ink poured across paper. But her look pleased Master no end.

She woke up one morning with a sudden clarity. Wait a minute, she thought. Her last period had been in early August—she was late! Could she be pregnant already?

It shouldn't be a surprise to her. She'd been fucked regularly now once or twice a day for the last three weeks—of course she'd get pregnant! Since she wasn't allowed to speak, she had no way of telling Master, so she decided to let him figure it out. She would need medical care and that might give her an opportunity to move to more comfortable quarters. She didn't like the idea of staying in the barn during the winter. Somehow, she imagined herself taken into Master's home and given a warm bed. But cows don't sleep in beds! What was she thinking? The most he might do is give her an extra blanket.

Over the next few weeks, she could feel her belly swell, although it would be imperceptible to the men. But they'd find out soon enough. For one, her breasts would get even larger. And she might get morning sickness. The only other change that she noticed early on was that she grew increasingly horny. She eagerly climbed into the milking frame and propped her big ass up for Bull, happy to feel his large cock stroking into her. Her orgasms grew in intensity and Bessie doubted she could ever go a day without at least a two or three strong ones.

Master began to watch her more closely and she suspected the light was finally dawning on him. It took another week for him to become convinced. When she threw up out in the pasture right after her morning milking he came over to make sure she didn't have the flu and recognized the symptoms.

"Hey, you're pregnant, aren't you?"

She looked up at him and nodded.

He clapped his hands. "Congratulations! Bull will be really excited to hear."

Bessie wondered if he even had the capacity to understand about pregnancy, but she kept her mouth shut, as usual.

Her life improved considerably after that day. Master made sure the heater was working properly and provided her with *two* extra blankets. Her meals became even larger. He also brought her vitamins that she took daily to give the growing baby all the nutrients it needed.

Bull, as she had suspected, didn't understand, and continued to fuck her as if nothing had changed. Master tried to get him to slow down, for the rocking motions often made her ill in the frame. He had to remove the chin pad and allow her head to hang down, braced only by a strap on her forehead, so she could vomit into a bucket below whenever she needed to.

As the weeks passed, her morning sickness went away and her stomach continued to swell. Bull finally seemed to understand that something was changing and didn't fuck her more than once a day now. Bessie found she missed it, despite her concern that the sex might somehow harm her unborn child.

She knew her life would be changing now. She couldn't quite understand how she could give birth and not be allowed to raise the child herself. Master said he would raise it. Surely they would need her milk? Her breasts ached with the thought of the baby suckling her. It would be far better than this machine!

But those questions were not for her to answer. She had her place and she was mostly content. It surprised her that she could achieve a state of grace about her position. In a way, it was a dream come true, although not exactly the script she would have written for herself.

Master led her out to the pasture, where the early fall sun still warmed the grass for her naked body to lie on. The dirt and the extra fat she carried now helped to insulate her. She knew, within the next few months, she'd have to be given something to wear when she was outside. Perhaps an old blanket, if nothing else. Master would want to protect her now that she was carrying his son's baby. She was glad she didn't have to worry about such things. She only had to eat and drink and be milked and fucked.

Master unhooked the leash from her nose ring and patted her on the head. "Good cow," he said.

"Mooooo," she responded, smiling up at him.

Printed in Great Britain
by Amazon

41810858R00116